MW01173344

"Con
hun
requ
bought the book based on its title
and those who seek a skillfully
written hard-boiled adventure tale
featuring page turner suspense and
characters of much greater depth
than one typically meets in books
aimed the sexual titillation market."
—Bill Kelly

"Conrad Dawn was an ex-sailor,
ex-fighter, ex-newspaper man, as
well as an ex-Marine… [he] had the
background and lived the life to
write these kinds of wild action
books true and accurate —
and kick-ass!"
—Gary Lovisi from his introduction

Conrad Dawn Bibliography
(1933-2002)

Chartered Love (1960)
Oriental Orgy (1960)
Amazon Lover (1961)
Too Much Broad (1961)
Any Time Any Place (1962)
Irresistible Nympho (1962)

CHARTERED LOVE

by Conrad Dawn

Introduction by Gary Lovisi

Black Gat Books • Eureka California

CHARTERED LOVE

Published by Black Gat Books
A division of Stark House Press
1315 H Street
Eureka, CA 95501, USA
griffinskye3@sbcglobal.net
www.starkhousepress.com

CHARTERED LOVE
Originally published and copyright © 1960
by Novel Books, Inc., Chicago.

ISBN: 979-8-88601-113-5

Cover design by Jeff Vorzimmer, ¡caliente!design, Austin, Texas
Text design by Mark Shepard, shepgraphics.com
Proofreading by Bill Kelly

First Stark House Press/Black Gat Edition: November 2024

CHARTERED LOVE
& CONRAD DAWN

by Gary Lovisi

I have always been a collector of Novel Books, so I was intrigued when I came upon *Chartered Love* by Conrad Dawn (Novel Book #3506, from 1961, a paperback original). I knew that some of these books were actually hidden little gems and this one looked like it just might fit the bill. So I decided to find out.

Novel Books offered low class sleaze from the lowest depths of soft-core paperback sleazedom. Their titles and cover art were outrageous, and to some today might even seem offensive. The exploitation pin-up photos of wild gals on their covers—often having their hair colored in bizarre shades of green, yellow, or red— decades before women ever thought of doing that these days—was just bizarre. Novel packaged those cover images and titles with cheesy come on blurbs such as—**"Hey, Men! Have We Got a Book For You!"** and **"Come on Guys, here is a book written by a *real* man—for *real* men!"** And they were correct— these were books specially written, designed and marketed for men. These were books for working class men who were looking for some quick sex and titillation, and not too much serious thinking in their entertainment reading. There is nothing wrong with

that. Today, the books are the epitome of what we
mean when we call a book 'sleaze'.

This publisher was a low end sleaze paperback
outfit—and *outfit* is perhaps the accurate word here—
as Camera Arts, the publisher of Novel Books (and
Merit Books)—was owned by men who were rumored
to be associated with the Chicago Outfit—aka the
Chicago Mafia. Not very nice people. For instance,
when one editor at Novel Books was sent a letter by
author Bob Tralins demanding payment for 18 of his
books that was two years late, he was sent a letter
back that told him to, "Go to Hell!" In any case, I
wondered just what the book might be about. I looked
it over, and it did look interesting. I read some of the
blurbs, and they further intrigued me, so I decided to
read two or three pages—giving it a chance—but
figuring that after three pages I would throw it down
and never read another page. Well, boy was I wrong!

Chartered Love is the story of John Darrow, a rough
and tumble charter ship operator. He's a devil-may-
care guy, a hard drinker and a tough fighter. He is a
guy who knows all the ins and outs of the sea lanes
around The Philippines, Macao and South Asia and
has been working odd jobs there for years after the
war. When young beauty Elizabeth McClain hires him
for what is in effect a salvage job, he sees the money
and the girl and goes along with it. He has to take his
boat, the *Malacca Maid*, out to where a ship was sunk
by the Japanese in World War II. It is now about 15
years later and the ship, *Mary Owen* has been lost—
but it was lost with millions of dollars in gold bars!
No one knows where the ship went down, the log book

page telling where the ship was hit was torn out!

Then begins a deadly treasure hunting adventure in the wilds of the East Asia seas. In a way, it is an Indiana Jones type adventure, decades before Indy was ever dreamed of. Darrow and his boat and crew (one of the most interesting characters is the old salt, Bart Adams, Darrow's First Mate), take McClain, and her uncle, out to dive to the sunken ship. However, a wily pirate, Suto Hayama, is on their trail doing everything he can to steal the gold. When Hayama takes his own boat and follows Darrow's *Malacca Maid,* a wild fighting battle through the Far East seas ensues. It is a rousing adventure, with a heroic cast of characters, and some twists and turns, before the story comes to a satisfying conclusion.

Chartered Love is a real sleeper in the Novel Books series by a fine pulp adventure writer. It is a great find! I don't want to give away too much here. It is a rousing adventure story, with interesting characters, set in an area of the world that has always been little known and mysterious to most readers. Author Conrad Dawn seems to know that part of the world very well, as well as the people and the landscape, the islands and the sea life and it comes through in the books. He gives us a very well-done adventure novel. While the book is packaged as a 1960s sleaze paperback, the story also features a rough-and-tumble love story between hard-boiled Darrow and sexy hard-headed Elizabeth set in exotic locales among interesting people full of danger and suspense. It even has some good qualities of a classic noir novel that would have made a good Bogart film.

So, while not exactly a sleaze tale, this Novel Book was certainly created to appeal to men, and men seemed to enjoy reading them. I can see why they sold pretty well too. Novel also had a reliable stable of professional writers who could put out tough guy fiction mixed with liberal doses of soft-core sex—though that 'sex' is timid and very mild by today's standards.

Reliable professionals who were considered lower-tier authors, only because they wrote in the paperback soft-core ghetto of the 1960s, did some fine work. Novel Books authors who wrote under their own name included: (Big) Bob Tralins; Ennis Willie (a hardboiled crime master, and a printer in Georgia); Jack Lynn; Duane Rimel (a well-known science fiction author who retired to Florida); Arnold Marmor from Queens, New York (whom I knew and published in my magazine *Hardboiled*); and George H. Smith (Harmon, not Henry). In fact, three of these authors I knew personally. Many of the authors of Novel Books did not write under a pseudonym or house name. Many used their own name. Some of these authors also had their photos on the back covers of their books—often posing with a weapon, or weapons. You see, that was the publisher's signal to let onto male book buyers these authors were *manly men*! Tough guys with guns? Probably, but it was a different era back then. However, many of these authors were World War II or Korea War vets, and *proud* of the fact. So I had a strong feeling that Conrad Dawn was the author's real name, and not some pseudonym or house name.

But who was Conrad Dawn? Well, that is the question. There is not much known about him at all. Judging by his photos, and the bios on the back cover of two of his Novel Books, that is most all we know. So he was 31 years old at the time he wrote *Chartered Love* in 1961. So here is the lowdown on him from those two book back covers. Did Novel Books play fast and loose with the facts? Perhaps? However, some of their books had author bios on the back covers and they were accurate—as attested to by other authors.

In fact, Conrad William Dawn was his actual name. His U.S. Marine Corps data tell us he was born December 9, 1933 in San Francisco, California and died on November 12, 2002 in Pima, Arizona. Dawn was a U.S. Marine from 1951 to 1954 in the Signal Corps, and was wounded in action in Korea on May 28, 1953. He was also married three times. So he certainly had experience in military matters, and it also seems with women.

The two book photos show us Dawn as a young, tough, lean, cowboy-looking guy, who it says traveled around the world more than once—hence his first-hand knowledge of the waters around Asia. His bio says he writes, "Manly, shocking fiction that hits harder than truth because it's based on the truth. Conrad Dawn has been around, guys, he writes what he's seen, and he's seen a helluva lot!"

Conrad Dawn was an ex-sailor, ex-fighter, ex-newspaper man, as well as an ex-Marine who in 1961 lived in Arizona. It is said he traveled six months a year to live 'man' material for his wild books. His bio adds, "You know that Dawn's words have the ring of truth to them, that he isn't some half-baked, bearded effeminate who loves his women or fights his brawls only on a typewriter. Dawn writes for Novel Books only."

I think that about sums it up. Conrad Dawn had the background and lived the life to write these kinds of wild action books true and accurate—*and kick-ass!*

So, come on, men!
You men asked us for it!
So here is the newest Novel Book!
Hey you guys (and gals)—this is a book for you!
Enjoy!

—Brooklyn, New York
April 28, 2024

....

Gary Lovisi has been nominated for a Mystery Writers of America Edgar Award for his crime fiction, and has won a Western Writers of America Spur Award as editor. He is the founder of Gryphon Books, the editor of *Paperback Parade* magazine, and the author of over twenty-five books including hardboiled thrillers, mysteries, Sherlock Holmes pastiches, science fiction and fantasy adventures, pulp fiction, plus non-fiction homages to the pulp world.

CHARTERED LOVE

LOVE

by Conrad Dawn

CHAPTER ONE

The rain began to fall about noon, slowly at first. Small droplets that all but evaporated before they touched the earth. The steam rose in soft, windblown wisps from the cobblestone streets, from the tin roofs of the peasant huts along the water, from the hot tile crowns atop the temples, and from the bodies of the people themselves. People that had long since stopped caring whether it rained, or blew, or the sun shown, or the world stopped, or it didn't.

Gradually it grew from a gentle shower to a heavy downpour. The wind rose from a soft moan to a shrill scream that rattled the roofs and shook the buildings and picked the litter from the streets and swept it into the rising water in the gutters.

John Darrow sipped leisurely on his scotch and water as he watched the half-hearted efforts of the people to clear their shops from the streets and take them into the questionable cover of their leaky huts.

He shifted his gaze to the half-filled glass in his strong, brown hand, studied the pleasure promising liquid within and then, with an almost automatic movement, raised it to his lips and drained it.

For Darrow, the day was all planned in advance. He knew what he was going to do, where he was going to do it, and when he was going to stop.

He would start with a few highballs at the Shun Low. Wander down to the mah-jongg tables at De Christo's in the early evening, and then maybe, in the wee hours of the morning, a woman or two, or maybe three. It depended upon how much he drank and on his luck at the mah-jongg tables.

Darrow gestured with the empty glass and the waiter shuffled over to the table with a fresh drink. "Will that be all, Captain Darrow?"

"That's all for now, Chan Do." He pulled a battered wallet from the rear pocket of his white ducks and handed the waiter a bill. "No, wait a minute. I'd better fortify myself for tonight. Bring me a steak, Chan Do. I want the best steak in the house and make it medium rare."

Chan Do smiled knowingly. "I think the Captain is going to have big night tonight. You want Chan Do find pretty girl maybe? I have new contact since last time Captain Darrow in Macao. Very pretty girls. Chinese, Portuguese, White Russian, Dutch. For you, I give discount."

He studied Darrow while waiting an answer and he saw before him a big man. Two hundred pounds or more of bone and muscle. Grey eyes that missed little and yet revealed nothing of what they had seen. The leathery face was blackened by many years of sun and wind and above the face, a thick, half-inch stubble of black hair, flecked with grey at the close-cut temples. A man who, at thirty-four, knew the reefs, the atolls, the currents and the very secrets of the South China Sea as well as any man alive.

Darrow lighted a cigarette and pondered over it momentarily before answering. He massaged the day-old stubble on his chin with one hand and his smile displayed a perfect row of unusually white teeth. "I

may take you up on that, Chan Do. First let's have
the steak. After that I'm going to get rip-roaring drunk,
lose half my pay as usual at the mah-jongg tables and
then I'll be back. I'll be back with bells on."

Chan Do bowed slightly from the waist and shuffled
off in the direction of the kitchen. This would be a
good day he felt. If the steak was good, there would be
a sizeable tip. If the girls were good tonight, there
would be an even bigger tip. Captain John Darrow
was a man who appreciated quality and was willing
to pay well for the valuable services that Chan Do
performed.

The rain was falling in sheets outside the window
and Darrow watched it cascade in little rivulets from
the roof of the Shun Low, flow a half inch deep across
the cobblestoned sidewalks and join the rushing
torrent in the gutters to begin the final journey to its
rendezvous with the tossing waters of the sea.

Darrow felt a close kinship with the rain as he
watched it, for in many respects his life was charted
along much the same course. He had been born on
the sea, as was the rain. He would return to the land
at times, cascade through the streets of the towns,
never stopping, possibly detoured here and there but
always, like the rain, rushing thankfully back to the
sea that was his life.

In the harbor below the many ships of many nations
were rising and falling in the swells. Sampans, junks,
tugboats, freighters, tankers and a liner or two, drawn
together from all parts of the world by the greed, the
beauty, the mystery and the enchantment that was
Macao.

It wasn't difficult to pick out the graceful lines of the *Malacca Maid* from where Darrow sat. She was docked alongside Pier 33, the fresh whiteness of her new paint job making her stand out like a queen among the varied colored ships anchored around her. She was Darrow's ship and he was proud of her. More than that, he loved her. He knew every wonderful creak of her rigging straining in a high sea. The grind of her engines were as familiar to him as his own voice. He beat her when he was mad, caressed her when she pleased him and talked to her for hours when he was lonely. He had sailed her forty-eight feet of wood, metal and canvas through every channel, along every current, ahead of every trade wind and past every island, reef or atoll of the South China Sea. She was his ship, but more than that, she was his life.

Chan Do placed the thick redness of the tenderloin in front of him, finished the setting with side dishes of rice, potatoes, a dish of unknown sprouts and roots and a pot of steaming tea. He watched with a deep pleasure as Darrow tore into it hungrily, consuming it to the last morsel.

The tables at De Christo's were crowded as usual, maybe more so, and Darrow's luck was bad. He dropped two month's profits by midnight and retired to a small table in a corner.

A Chinese girl in a tight-fitting dress brought scotch and water and placed it on the table before him. She smiled enticingly and as she left, Darrow studied the artful wiggle of her back side with the true appreciation of a man that had spent the last three months at sea. He felt the warm glow rise up within him, engulfing his body and he knew it was time to embark upon the final stage of the night.

He lighted a cigarette and took a deep drag. What would it be tonight? The soft gentle ways of an almond-eyed Chinese beauty? The wild, uninhibited love making of a golden-haired White Russian, or the stormy, deep passion of one of the colony's many Portuguese or Spanish belles? To be sure, it was a problem not easily decided upon. Only one thing was certain, the night would be a joyful one, for tomorrow he would return to the *Malacca Maid* with a throbbing head, a growling stomach and an empty wallet. After that, it would be another three months or so at sea before he returned to start the cycle again.

He ordered a second drink and had almost finished it when the girl came in. He had been watching casually the flow of human traffic in and out of the front door. The people of Macao never ceased to interest him. In the past few minutes, he had seen Ramon Cantos, who had built a fortune in dope traffic; Alex Greer, a reward on his head in every British colony in the Far East; Suto Hayama, gun runner, smuggler, pirate and murderer. It had been an interesting flow of humanity, but the girl was the most fascinating by far.

She was small, but well proportioned. A hundred and ten pounds or so of perfectly distributed female flesh. Her jet-black hair was set in a stunning American fashion that hung almost to her shoulders.

A saucy nose was set perfectly on a slightly over-rounded face and the lights of De Christo's casino flashed brightly in her dark eyes as she looked uneasily around the room. A simple white suit accentuated the swell of her ample breasts and rounded buttocks.

She caught the eye of a bustling waiter and put her mouth close to his ear in order to be heard above the turmoil of dice, loud laughter and the clink of silver. The waiter listened, shook his head slightly and started to move off, but she caught his sleeve and pressed a bill into his hand. He stopped, pocketed the money, and pointed at Darrow's table.

She smiled her thanks and started over, her muscles rippling smoothly under the thin material of her suit.

Darrow was on his feet and had pulled out one of the ornately hand carved teak wood chairs before she was half way there. He waited until she had seated herself and then helped her move it closer to the table.

Her rose red lips formed in a fleeting smile of thanks and she searched through her white leather bag until she found her cigarettes. She opened them and offered one to Darrow, taking one herself after he refused. She accepted Darrow's hasty light and blew a stream of blue smoke into the already hazy atmosphere before she spoke. "I hope you're Captain Darrow. It would be rather embarrassing if you weren't."

Darrow seated himself opposite her and signaled the waiter for a drink before answering. "I'm Darrow. What can I do for you?" He grinned wickedly, running his eyes over the smooth contours of her body.

She must have guessed what had been crossing his mind because she flushed slightly and lowered her eyes. "It's strictly a business matter, Mr. Darrow. I suppose I should say, Captain Darrow." She hesitated for a second, uncertainly. "If you and your ship are available, it should be profitable for both of us. Very profitable."

Darrow picked one of his own cigarettes from a crumpled pack in his shirt pocket and lighted it. "Your name is ...?"

"I'm sorry. I'm Elizabeth McClain." She flushed again, but this time her eyes matched his, never wavering. The lady was very determined, Darrow decided.

"My ship may be for hire, Miss McClain. It depends on what for and for how much."

The waiter came with Darrow's scotch and water, set it down and looked inquiringly at Elizabeth McClain. She said to Darrow. "I'll have a gin and tonic. I need something in this heat."

Darrow repeated the order to the waiter and waited until he left before continuing. "How did you happen to come to me, Miss McClain, and after you chose me, how did you know I'd be here?"

"My uncle is Peter Vargas of Singapore, Captain. He told me that you would be the best man for what I have in mind. I went to your ship this evening and your mate said you would be here about this time."

Darrow knew Vargas from a few years ago. Vargas had been in the import-export business, specializing in Oriental and Polynesian furniture and curios. Darrow had delivered a few cargoes to him from the South Pacific right after the war, but that had been the extent of it. He was rather surprised to hear that Vargas had recommended him or even remembered him after so many years.

"Why do you want to charter the *Malacca Maid*, Miss McClain?"

"I would prefer not to say just yet. At least not until you refuse or accept my offer. What is your usual fee for say, three months?"

Darrow laughed inwardly, rather pleased with her caginess. It wasn't too often you met one with beauty and brains combined. "Is it legal?"

"It's legal, Captain. I can assure you of that. I understand from Uncle Peter though, that with John Darrow and his *Malacca Maid* it doesn't make much difference whether it's legal or not."

"Only in the price, Miss McClain. Only in the price." He fell silent for a moment. "It must be pretty important to bring you here at this time of night. How does four thousand a month sound?"

"That sounds fair enough to me, Captain, but I was thinking along terms of fifty percent of twelve million dollars."

CHAPTER TWO

Darrow whistled softly. "I thought you said it was legal. I didn't know there was that much honest money available."

"I only said it was legal. I didn't say it would be easy to come by."

"The *Malacca Maid* is at your service, Miss McClain. If you'd care to be at the ship in the morning, we can discuss the voyage and make the final preparations. I'll expect a four thousand guarantee in advance, of course. Now, if you'll excuse me, I have some things to do." He started to rise from the table.

Elizabeth McClain reached in her purse and pushed a roll of bills across the table. "There's five thousand dollars here. It's yours, but I'm afraid I'll need your immediate help, Captain."

Darrow looked at the money hungrily. "Now look, Miss. If you have any ideas about getting under way tonight, it's out of the question. We have to take on fuel and supplies, and I have a sail that needs mending. It will be tomorrow afternoon at the earliest." He reseated himself in the chair and pocketed the roll of bills before she changed her mind.

"That won't be necessary. My first need is for protection."

Darrow leaned back in his chair, not bothering to hide his impatience. He'd be damned if he would play nursemaid to some damn fool woman. Even for five thousand dollars. He was certain she was nothing more than a rattle-brained female with a wild imagination. It was true that Macao wasn't the safest place in the world for a Western woman, but then she had made it this far alone. "Now look, lady. I'm a sea captain. If it's a bodyguard you're looking for, you've come to the wrong man."

"Please, let me explain. Is there some place we can talk in private?"

Darrow snorted impatiently and rose from the table, kicking back his chair. "Come on. We can go in the back. The rooms back there aren't usually occupied by what you might call 'ladies,' but then I guess it won't kill you." He took her by the arm and led her, more gently than he would have liked to, through the crowd.

There was a small curtained door at the rear of the room and they headed for that. A young Chinese with a pockmarked face stood at the curtain and he winked when Darrow pressed the money into his hand. "You got a nice one tonight, Captain. I could go for a little of that myself."

Darrow didn't bother to explain. He pushed through the curtain into a dimly lighted hallway that ran for sixty feet and ended in a blank wall. On each side of the hall, sliding doors exited into the usual small rooms.

They found one that was open and Darrow stepped through, pushing her ahead of him. Elizabeth glanced at the simple bed, the washstand and the small table containing various items that one might need. If she had any doubt before as to where they were, she had none now. She blushed slightly and sat gingerly on the edge of the chair, no longer looking around, but keeping her eyes straight ahead.

Darrow slid the door shut behind them and stretched out comfortably on the bed. He thought of the last time he had been in that room. "Oh, what a doll!" he thought. She had been Chinese. Young, but wise in the ways of love. He realized suddenly that he was tired and more than a little drunk. "The atmosphere bother you, Miss McClain? I told you they didn't usually accommodate 'ladies' back here."

She continued to look straight ahead. "That man at the door. You didn't have to let him think—"

"Why not? You'll never see him again. Besides, these

rooms are rented for one thing and that one thing only. If he would have thought we wanted to use it for anything else, he might not have let us back here." He lighted his last cigarette and placed one arm behind his head to serve as a pillow. "You'd better get on with your story. I only paid for half an hour. Best you keep your voice down though. These walls are paper thin."

"All right, Captain." She crossed her legs, revealing a short glimpse of white thigh. "Have you ever heard of the *Mary Owen*?"

"Yes, I think so. She was sunk about 1938 or '39. If I recall correctly, she was carrying the last load of refugees from Canton just before the Japs moved in. She was bound for Australia, but the Japs caught up with her in the Sulu Sea and she was torpedoed. Not many survivors as I remember."

"You're right so far, Captain. The year was 1938 and there were six hundred passengers and a crew of fifty. There were thirty survivors." She stopped as if trying to recall the exact details, took a deep breath and went on. "My father was Second Mate of the *Mary Owen*. He drifted at sea for eighteen days before he was picked up. Last month he died. But before he died, he told me a story that only two people in the world know the truth of. Among the passengers on the *Mary Owen*, was a general in the Chinese Army. A man called Chang Tse Tung. That is common knowledge. What isn't known is that when General Chang boarded the *Mary Owen*, he brought aboard about twelve million dollars in gold bars."

Darrow whistled softly. "How did your father know

this?" He was beginning to be swept up in the excitement that had shaken Elizabeth's voice.

"He supervised the loading. He was suspicious at the weight of the crates and after they were at sea, he broke them open. He calculated from the weight that there was roughly twelve million there. At any rate, when they were torpedoed, Dad was in the chart room. When the order came to abandon ship, he tore the last page from the ship's log. Their position had been entered just before the torpedo struck. He intended to go back after the gold as soon as he could raise the money for salvage operations. Then came Pearl Harbor. He joined the Merchant Marine in 1942 and was torpedoed twice more. By the time the war was over, he was a sick man. He never did get back." Her voice had fallen to little more than a whisper by this time and there were tears in her eyes.

Darrow was sitting bolt upright now, stone sober and alert. "Do you have quick access to that page from the log?"

Elizabeth McClain reached inside her white jacket and fumbled in the area of her breasts. Then, realizing that Darrow was watching, slightly bug-eyed, turned away. She turned back after a moment and handed a wrinkled paper to him. "My brassiere was the safest place I could think of to carry it. I think now that it will be safer with you."

Darrow took the paper eagerly and studied its half-completed face. It was brown and worn with age, was tearing at the folds and the ink had run quite badly, but most of the writing was legible. The last entry was made at 0600. The position had been 120 degrees,

6 minutes East by 8 degrees, 4 minutes North. Bearing had been S.S.E. at eighteen knots.

"Well, we have her last position here. With any luck, we should be able to find where she went down, but that doesn't mean we can get at her. Those waters can get pretty deep. Do you know how long after the last entry was made that she went down?"

"My father said she was hit at 0604 and she went under at about 0615. Dad said that with these coordinates, we could narrow it down to an area about a half mile square." Elizabeth rose and walked nervously around the room.

"You said that you needed my protection. You haven't told anyone else about this?"

"No, of course not! But somehow or other, someone knows, or at least suspects, that I have something. Shortly after Dad died, our home in San Francisco was ransacked. On the way over here, my cabin on the ship was searched and a steward was killed. The thought was that he surprised someone in the act. Finally, I'm quite sure I was followed here tonight."

Darrow slipped the paper inside his shirt and went to the door, sliding it open. The hall was empty. He turned back to Elizabeth. "I think we'd better go to the *Malacca Maid*. I'd like to put this paper in the ship's safe and I think you'd be better off there too. I'll send my Mate after your luggage first thing in the morning."

She nodded her agreement and he helped her through the door ahead of him. He grinned sheepishly at the doorman and tossed him another coin on the way out.

CHAPTER THREE

They pushed their way through the swarming crowd and stepped out onto the darkened street. The storm had passed, but the cobblestones were still slippery and now and then it was necessary to sidestep the puddles that still remained in the street.

Darrow looked for a rickshaw or cab as they moved, but there was none to be had. As they came closer to the waterfront, the streets were all but deserted. An occasional drunk could be seen sleeping one off in a darkened doorway or back alley and now and then, the sounds of laughter or song would reach their ears.

The rain had quelled the heat of the day and as they walked, Darrow sucked great breaths of the fresh night air into his lungs. A light flashed on the street ahead from an open doorway and gay laughter echoed from within. It was the time of night for frivolity and Darrow was beginning to regret that she had found him so soon. He decided that had Elizabeth not come, he would have chosen one of the Chinese girls for the remainder of the night. That waitress in the tight dress had turned the trick in the favor of her race.

They rounded the last corner and started down the row of warehouses to Pier 33. The moon broke through the clouds for a split second, lighting up the street ahead and Darrow jumped into the shadows, pulling Elizabeth with him. Had it been his mind playing tricks? No! Something had moved. Against the warehouse a few yards ahead! It disappeared when he looked directly at it, but by turning his head a little to one side, he could barely make out the darker shapes against the darkened wall.

He searched the ground around them for a weapon of some sort, but there was none to be had. They would have to go on regardless.

They stepped out of the shadows and into the middle of the street. "If something happens, you make a run for the ship. I'll stand them off as best I can." He removed the log page from his shirt and pressed it into her hand. "When you get there, holler like hell for the First Mate and tell him what's going on. If they get through me and catch you before you can reach the ship, give them the paper. They wouldn't think twice about killing you for it."

"I'll not leave you to fight my battles. I'm staying. There must be something I can do."

"You do as I tell you, or it's curtains for both of us."

They were getting closer now and as they came alongside the spot where he had seen the movement, three forms stepped from the shadows. The moon broke through the clouds again and a knife flashed in the hand of the nearest one.

"All right, lady. Get the hell out of here." He shoved Elizabeth hard in the direction of the ship and balanced himself on the balls of his feet as the men closed in. One of them made a dash for Elizabeth and Darrow moved at the same time. His flying tackle caught the man dead center and they tumbled to the cobblestones in, a heap of flying fists and elbows. He struck out hard with his right hand and grunted with satisfaction as his fist sank wrist deep into the man's mid-section.

A pair of sinewy arms circled his throat from behind and stars began to flash before his eyes as his air supply was cut off. He struggled to his feet with the man on his back and once there, stepped to one side and lashed a backward blow at the man's groin. There was a scream of agony and the arms loosened their grip.

Darrow felt a sharp stab of pain in his left shoulder and that arm went limp. He spun around to face the third man and the knife flashed again. He threw up his right arm and caught the man's wrist in a vise-like grip. He twisted hard and the knife clattered to the street. He dove for it but before he could regain his feet, there were two men on his back and his face was being forced roughly into the pavement.

He twisted to one side and buried the knife to the hilt in someone's rib cage. The body went limp and he pushed it off, but couldn't retrieve the weapon. Something landed in a glancing blow on the side of his head and ricocheted off onto the injured shoulder, sending a stab of pain through his whole body. He struck out blindly and missed, the momentum carrying him face down on the cobblestones once more.

They were atop him again and he knew he was losing the fight. Someone grabbed his right arm and jerked it up sharply behind his back. Strong fingers grabbed at this throat and he felt himself slipping slowly off into darkness.

When Darrow came to, the world was spinning wildly and a series of strange faces with no bodies floated before him. His body ached from one end to the other, his throat was raw, and when he attempted to move his left arm, there was no response. He coughed harshly and his chest burned like the fires of hell. His mouth filled with blood and when he swallowed, he rolled to one side immediately and threw it back up.

Someone wiped his eyes and forehead with a damp cloth and then a glass was forced between his bruised lips and he choked when the liquor tried to go down. He could vaguely hear voices mumbling in the distance, but they made no sense.

He tried opening his eyes again. This time the spinning wasn't as bad and the faces gradually came into focus. It was Elizabeth McClain. "Good God! They got her after all," he thought. "No ... no, they hadn't. The other face. Who was it? Strangely familiar. Barton Adams. Good old Bart. The best First Mate a Captain ever had!" His body was tense. Tense as a watch spring and when he recognized Adams, he relaxed. His body went limp and he felt the darkness rush over him again.

When he regained consciousness the next time, the spinning had stopped altogether. He moved his head painfully and saw that the sunlight was streaming brightly through the porthole. The smell of freshly made coffee drifted past his nostrils and his stomach growled loudly, signaling his hunger. "Hey! Mr. Adams, bring me some of that damn lousy coffee of yours."

He tried to raise himself, but the pain shot through his left shoulder again, forcing him to lie back. "Adams! Damn it, Adams, get your hind end in here."

The mahogany door slid open after a few seconds

and Bart Adams stepped in with a mug of steaming black coffee. He scratched a sunburned, bald head with his free hand and surveyed Darrow critically.

Satisfied that he was completely conscious and well on the road back to normal, he chuckled good naturedly and set the coffee beside the bunk. "I got to say one thing for you, Cap'n. When you get yourself in trouble, you don't do no halfway job of it. Damn good thing you got an able-bodied crew. They was about ready to cut you in little pieces and feed you to the fishes when we barged in."

Darrow tried again and this time managed to sit up, ignoring the pain. "Elizabeth McClain. Is she all right?"

"I guess she'll make it O.K. A little shook up last night, but she's poundin' her ear now. Spunky little wench wouldn't go to bed until just a few minutes ago. Wanted to wait until she was sure you was all right. I tried to tell her you was far too ornery to cash in so damn young and even if you did, wouldn't nobody miss you much. I explained how it's really me what keeps this leaky tub in business."

It was Darrow's turn to chuckle now. "Good for you, Bart. Like you said, it's a damn good thing I've got a good crew." He took the cup and lifted it to his lips. The first mouthful he swished gently between his teeth, then allowed it to seep slowly down his throat. It burned when it hit the raw spots, but in comparison to the rest of his body, it was pure ecstasy. He swung his legs slowly over the side of the bunk and rested his back against the bulkhead, while he finished the remainder of the coffee. His strength was gradually returning and by the time the coffee was gone he felt pretty good, all things being what they were.

He set the cup down and stepped carefully onto his feet. He grabbed Adams until the room stopped spinning, then tested his left arm. It was weak, stiff and more than a little sore, but he figured it would do. "What happened after you boys butted in last night, Bart?"

Adams strolled to a chair against the opposite bulkhead and eased himself into it. He pulled a battered pipe from a hip pocket and, taking a pouch from the other, began to fill it slowly. He tamped the last bit of tobacco into place and struck a match on the underside of the chair, watching the flame grow to its peak before touching it to the pipe.

He sucked loudly a few times until the blue smoke began to curl toward the open porthole, then pitched the match through into the water. "Well, there isn't much to tell. We found this one bastard deader 'n hell with a sticker in his ribs and these other two boys was just startin' to go to work on you." He stopped to suck again on the pipe. "Anyway, we felt obligated to cut in, you bein' our skipper and all that. One of 'em got his neck broke somehow and the other one took off like a bat out o' hell. I suppose the fish got the bones of the two dead ones pretty well picked clean by this time. Seems like I saw a couple o' shark fins under the pier just before dark last night."

Darrow expressed his satisfaction at their night's work and stepped through the door, then climbed slowly to the deck. The brightness of the sunlight hurt his eyes and he shaded them with his hand until they became accustomed to the glare. He walked to the rail and leaned against it shakily, staring down at the litter-filled waters. A seagull darted down from nowhere and came up with a small fish that had been feeding on some nearby garbage. Beyond the garbage, numerous jelly fish floated lazily on the surface.

Back on the stern of the *Malacca Maid*, Joe Apiki and Kevin O'Mally spliced a worn-out line and eyed Darrow curiously. He waved to them and flashed a white-toothed smile. "Thanks, boys. I won't forget what you did last night."

He turned to the port side and watched a junk sail gracefully into the crowded harbor, its bow cutting sharply into the calm waters and setting the smaller boats to rocking in their mooring. He was thinking of what Elizabeth had told him last night. It was unbelievable. Too good to be true and yet the story was completely plausible.

Darrow picked a cigarette from his shirt pocket, lighted it and flipped the match into the water. In his lifetime, he must have heard a hundred stories of sunken treasure. Of those, probably only five or ten percent were based on the merest semblance of fact.

Elizabeth had given him five thousand dollars in advance last night, though. People didn't go around spending that kind of money unless they were reasonably sure of themselves. He glowered at the deck. There was someone else that thought the gold existed too. That was pretty well confirmed last night.

Elizabeth had said that two people had known the truth of the *Mary Owen*'s cargo. She would be one. Who was the other person?

General Chang Tse Tung perhaps? Had he survived the wreck? Elizabeth hadn't said. He tried to recall further details about the General without too much success. Anything that he remembered hearing of the man's life had taken place prior to the sinking. If he was alive, he had certainly drifted into obscurity. Biding his time possibly, waiting for the right moment to strike.

He scratched his chin meditatively. If it was Chang, the chances were that he would not have the exact coordinates of the sinking. Had he suspicioned that McClain would know? Perhaps watching him secretly for years, waiting for him to make a move. The idea was far-fetched, but possible. A man could afford to wait seventeen years when the stakes were this high.

Barton Adams leaned patiently against the rail at Darrow's side. His pipe had gone out and he struck a match to it, his eyes studying Darrow closely. His grizzled features betrayed his curiosity about last night's happenings, but he said nothing.

Darrow turned to Adams. "How does our diving gear stack up? Pretty poor shape, I guess."

"Not too bad, Cap'n. Our compressor needs a little work and the suit could use a few patches. Nothing that couldn't be taken care of in a day or so. We got us a little salvage job lined up?"

Darrow chose to let the question pass for the time being and remained silent, continuing to watch the busy early morning activities of the harbor. The diving gear that they had would be fine once they had located the wreck. It was of the old-fashioned type. Fed from the compressor on the surface, but having the distinct advantage of allowing the diver to remain below for long periods of time. For a search that might very well have to cover a half mile or better of ocean bottom, however, it was far too cumbersome.

"Have O'Mally start to work on the air compressor this morning, Bart. We're going to be needing it before too long. Then, this afternoon, I want you to go ashore and pick up two sets of SCUBA gear with extra tanks. Have the boys bring aboard enough supplies for ninety days. We're getting under way the first thing tomorrow morning."

"Aye, aye, Skipper. The girl going with us?"

"She is." He took a final puff on the cigarette and dropped it into the water. "I'm going ashore now. When Miss McClain wakes up, don't let her leave the ship under any condition. I might not be back until late, so I'm depending on you to have the ship ready to sail at dawn."

Adams slapped an inquisitive fly off of his shoulder with a raw-boned hand. "Good as done, Cap'n. I'll see you tonight then."

Darrow nodded acknowledgment and stepped onto the dock. He walked two blocks before he found and waved down a rickshaw. The slim Chinese lifted the yoke and half turned, waiting for instructions as Darrow climbed stiffly into the seat. "The House of Yang She. You go fast. Chop chop. I pay extra."

In his years in the Orient, Darrow had picked up two dialects of Chinese, enough Japanese to get by on and a workable knowledge of Portuguese, but he had found in the past, that it was wise to use it only when necessary. The value of understanding the language far exceeded that of speaking it.

The coolie trotted off at a good pace and Darrow relaxed against the hot leather padding of the seat. They rumbled over the cobblestone streets of the waterfront area, past the rows of casinos and bars and then out onto the tree lined Avenieda Almieda Ribeiro, the main shopping and tourist center of Macao. The streets were already filled with rickshaws, autos and milling crowds and the coolie swore miserably at them in Chinese, as he yelled at them to clear the way before him.

The House of Yang She was in the center of the island, a good thirty-minute ride from the docks. That would allow, Darrow figured, plenty of time for him to coordinate his thoughts and for the hundred-some-odd girls to awaken after a busy night.

Yang She's was the largest, most popular, and best brothel on the island. That is, they had the best. They also had the cheapest. The price of a girl ranged all the way from one Hong Kong dollar (about sixteen cents, American), to the price of a new car. There was one entrance for the well-to-do and the tourist trade and another for the lowly coolie. Both doors were filled with traffic from dark till dawn.

It wasn't a girl that Darrow was after, however. Adams had taken six hundred Hong Kong dollars from the body of one of the Chinese last night. They had evidently been paid in advance for the job and there was still one man running loose in Macao. Darrow wanted him. If he held true to form, he'd be out spending that money, and Yang She's was the best spot to start looking.

They passed the beautiful gardens of Kwan Yin Tong, the Temple of the Goddess of Mercy, and ahead of them, Penha Hill loomed against the sky. Beyond this hill, was Communist China and at the peak of the hill, was the House of Yang She.

The coolie dropped the cart at the door and showed a mouthful of broken and rotted teeth, when Darrow paid him off. He would expect a handsome cut from Yang She also. The directing of business to the House of Yang She was far more profitable than just pulling a rickshaw.

The heavy door was locked from within and Darrow yanked the bell cord impatiently, waiting perhaps two or three minutes before it opened.

A teenaged houseboy in an immaculate white jacket showed him through into the richly carpeted hall and bade him be seated. A girl would be down in a few minutes. "I don't want a girl, fella," he said. "Tell Yang She that John Darrow is here."

CHAPTER FOUR

Darrow seated himself on the long couch in the lobby and lighted a cigarette as the houseboy hurried off down the hall and up the winding stairway to the second floor.

He tugged gently at his left ear and then ran his fingers across the stubble of black hair. He had known Yang She since she had been a not too innocent girl of twenty. That would have been about eight years he thought. She had come a long ways since then. Their friendship had been one of warmth and pleasantness and Darrow looked back on it with many happy memories.

"John! John Darrow!" She had come up behind him silently and wrapped her lovely arms about his neck, her long black hair brushing gently against his face.

He turned sharply and pain flicked across his face momentarily as the injured shoulder was twisted too quickly. "Hello, Yang She. It's been a while."

"Too long, John. Much too long. I begin to feel that you are ashamed to be known as the friend of Yang She." Her lips were formed in a feminine pout, but her eyes flashed with merriment as she looked at the face of her old friend.

"You know better than that. It has been too long, but the next interval will be shorter, I promise." He smiled warmly as he took her hand.

She led the way up the stairs, refusing to let go of his hand and all the time, filling his ears with chatter. She turned right at the top of the stairs and opened a door at the end of the hall. The room was large and expensively furnished. A deep carpet extended from wall to wall, spotted here and there with the low Oriental tables. An American influence was present also in the large picture window that overlooked the harbor and in the huge, canopied bed that could be seen in the adjoining room.

Yang She seated herself upon one of the light cushions in front of the window and motioned for Darrow to join her. Her robe slid aside as she sat and Darrow noticed that she was naked beneath it.

"Come, John. Sit beside me. There is room enough

for two ... almost. Sit, but say nothing. Let me look at you for a moment."

Darrow sat and as he did so, his hand touched her leg where her robe had parted. He let it linger momentarily, then pulled it away, not knowing quite what to do with it. Yang She was right. The pillow was large enough for both of them ... almost.

Yang She looked at him, her face puzzled. "Why do you move your hand, John Darrow? I think maybe you have grown tired of Yang She. You think that she is but one of the girls that she employs. I swear to you. I have not had a man since last I saw you. More than a year ago." She was serious now. Serious and slightly hurt by Darrow's actions.

"I'm sorry, Yang She. It's not that and you know it. It's just that I'm here on business and it doesn't take too much on your part for me to decide to let business go to hell." He lighted a cigarette and handed it to her, then took one for himself.

The answer seemed to satisfy her for the puzzled took disappeared and she giggled softly. Her own hand crept teasingly to Darrow's thigh and she squeezed it gently. "What is your business, John? If your request is within Yang She's power it is as good as granted."

"I'm looking for someone, Yang She. A Chinese. Fairly young. Maybe a fisherman or a coolie. If he came here, it would have been sometime after one o'clock this morning. He would have been flashing a roll of bills big enough to choke a horse, unless I miss my guess. A hell of a lot more than you would expect someone of his class to have." Darrow flicked his ashes in the tray on the table before them. "I want this man. I want him bad."

Yang She picked a bell from the table and jingled it softly. A door opened almost immediately and the houseboy shuffled before them. She repeated Darrow's request to the boy and he moved off as quickly as he had come, closing the door behind him.

"It will take a while, John. Perhaps an hour or better. Some of the girls are still sleeping. Others have left to spend the day with their families. They will be hard to find." She rose gracefully to her feet and stepped to the window. "I can see the whole harbor from here, John. I saw the *Malacca Maid* come in three days ago. I was hoping you would come see me."

Darrow mashed his cigarette out in the ashtray and, getting to his feet, moved over beside her. Yang She turned to face him and let the robe slide from her shoulders and fall in a crumpled heap at her feet. The morning sun beamed in through the window and accentuated the bronzed tones of her slim body. Her breasts began to rise and fall gently as her breathing quickened.

Darrow let his eyes skim quickly over her body, from the tiny feet to the rounded hips to the swell of her breasts.

She let him stare hungrily for a second, then stepped forward and hooked one golden arm around his neck, her pointed breasts thrust against his chest. Her ruby lips parted in a silent moan of pleasure, then rose to meet his.

A warm glow spread over Darrow, as her hands caressed his body. He lifted her in his arms in one swift motion, the injured shoulder all but forgotten in the passion of the moment. A few rapid strides to the adjoining room and they were side by side on the large bed.

Yang She, hands trembling with excitement, removed his clothing tenderly and then, all tenderness gone, threw herself at him with a passion that only a woman such as Yang She can know.

Her lovely legs, her slim arms opened to engulf him and they found themselves swept suddenly into the dark, infinite, pleasure filled abyss of life.

When it was over, he lay on his back staring lazily at the canopy above the bed. He felt as though the whole world could go to hell now. He always felt this way after being with Yang She.

Darrow could hear her washing in the bathroom and he cursed himself under his breath for allowing such thoughts to enter his mind. There was still a job to be done.

Swinging his legs over the side of the bed, he began to dress quickly and by the time she returned, he was seated in the living room sucking nervously on a cigarette.

It was obviously over and the disappointment showed in her eyes, clouding over the joy that had been there only minutes before. "You must go soon, John."

"I'm sorry, Yang She." He walked over and kissed her softly. "I told you I was here on business. You don't know how much I want to stay though." He tapped her on the chin gently with his big fist and turned away, not wanting to see the look on her face.

There was nothing more to say and therefore, there

was silence until the houseboy returned minutes later. The boy's face was impassive, revealing nothing of what he had learned.

Darrow snorted impatiently. "Well?"

Rather than answer, the boy beckoned Yang She to one side and whispered briefly in her ear. She answered softly in Chinese and the boy left the room.

"I'm afraid I have some bad news for you, John. I think we have found your man." She hesitated slightly. "He came in last night at three o'clock, ordered a bottle of wine and one of our better rooms. He wanted a white girl, but was refused. Instead, we gave him one of the cheaper girls, put her in a nice room and charged him ten times the usual price. He was stupid and it seemed to satisfy him."

She stopped again and Darrow said, "Go on, go on. That sounds like it might be the one. What do you mean, bad news?"

"I think you had better come with me, John. There has been some trouble."

She left the room hurriedly with Darrow at her heels. They moved through the halls to the back of the building and then down two flights of stairs to the basement. A row of numbered doors lined the north side and Yang She picked one and unlocked it.

The room was small but neat and the two people on the bed might have been sleeping. They might have been, but they weren't. The single sheet that covered their naked bodies had been pulled back and they were still locked in each other's arms. Beneath them, their life's blood had mixed in a single pool that saturated the bedding and was now dripping slowly, drop by drop, onto the cement floor. Darrow counted a total of seven bullet holes in their two bodies.

"My boy found them this way a few minutes ago, John. No one heard anything this morning, so whoever did it must have used a silencer."

"Well, that's my man. I couldn't have been sure before, but this clinches it." He backed out, closing the door, and lighted a cigarette nervously. "He failed in his job and this is what he got for it. Do you know him, Yang She?"

"My houseboy says he is a pirate. One of Suto Hayama's men. This was found in his clothes." She handed Darrow a roll of bills. "There is three hundred dollars here. He paid three hundred twenty for the girl."

Darrow looked at the money in his hands, gathering his thoughts. Suto Hayama. A dangerous man to reckon with. As bad as any on the island. He returned the money to Yang She and added more of his own. "Give this to the girl's parents. I'm sorry this had to happen here. Will you be in bad trouble?"

"I think not. This has never happened here before, but it will pass. The authorities might close us down for a few days, but we will reopen. It is the girl that I feel sorry for. She was a pretty thing." Yang She leaned weakly against the wall, her face downcast, her body drained of strength.

Darrow squeezed her arm reassuringly and kissed her on the cheek. "If you run into trouble, call me. I'll be leaving tomorrow at dawn, if things go well. If they don't, another day or so won't matter." He embraced her tenderly and left, climbing into a passing taxi.

CHAPTER FIVE

He knew who he was dealing with now. At least partly so. Suto Hayama was big in Macao, but his operations were limited mostly to that area. There had to be someone else. Someone above Hayama that had extended the search from San Francisco to the Orient.

As it stood now, though, the best thing they could do was run. Hayama commanded three junks and perhaps a hundred men. More if he needed them. The only thing to do was make for the open sea and take a chance on out distancing them.

Maybe there was something he could do. It was against Darrow's nature to run from a fight and, even if he couldn't afford to engage them full scale, a parting shot would be sweet revenge for the beating he had suffered the night before. A plan began to slowly formulate in his mind and the more he thought about it the better he liked it.

He had ordered the driver to head for the waterfront and now they were almost there. At Darrow's direction, the driver swerved sharply down a narrow alley to their left and careened dangerously through the milling crowds and peddlers' carts, scattering them with blasts of his horn.

They continued on for perhaps ten minutes, twisting in and out of the streets and alleys until they came to a long, dirty-grey warehouse in the factory district. Darrow tapped the driver on the shoulder and they screeched to a halt at the far end of the building.

"Ah, Captain Darrow. It is nice to see you again. Perhaps you have a cargo of guns for Wah Hang?" The man greeted Darrow at the door, shaking his hand warmly and then backing off in anticipation. "We're pretty well stocked at present, but perhaps I can take them off your hands at somewhat less than the usual price. It would be dangerous for you to hold them too long."

Darrow had always disliked Wah Hang and made no effort to hide the fact. Looking at the man now, he liked him even less than usual, but out of necessity, he would have to use him. "I'm glad to hear that you're well stocked, Wah Hang, because I'm here to buy rather than sell. I'll have four cases of TNT and some underwater time fuse. About a hundred feet should do it."

Wah Hang was eager now, the prospects of a good sale were pleasant at this time. He barked an order to a waiting laborer and the man disappeared behind the rows of draperies and Oriental rugs that served as a front for the biggest sales place of smuggled guns and ammunition on Macao. Shortly the order was wheeled to the front.

"Will there be anything else, Captain?" He was figuring rapidly on a piece of brown wrapping paper.

"There will. I want a Browning Automatic Rifle and five thousand rounds of ammunition. Better give me two thousand rounds of .45 caliber ammunition. That ought to do it."

The *Malacca Maid* already carried a Thompson sub-machine gun and two forty-five automatics. In a possible running fight with one of Hayama's junks, however, the long range of the BAR could well mean the difference between life and death.

The request was filled and Wah Hang continued to figure on the paper. "That will be nine hundred and fifty dollars, Captain Darrow."

"You're crazy, Wah Hang. I'll give you five hundred." He peeled off the bills and threw them on the counter, then walked out leaving Wah Hang screaming shrilly in Chinese, his face distorted and his arms waving wildly in the air.

Darrow climbed in the cab and checked his watch. It was two o'clock. They were well ahead of schedule. If things went the way they should, the *Malacca Maid* would be well out to sea by dawn and Suto Hayama, if he was still alive, would be considerably the worse for having tangled with John Darrow.

Elizabeth McClain had changed from the white suit of the evening before into shorts and blouse. She greeted Darrow warmly from her seat on the forward hatch and set aside the sailcloth she had been mending. "They're bound and determined to make a sailor out of me, Captain. Darned if it isn't something like keeping house." She laughed jauntily and Darrow was pleased to note that some of the tension of last night had gone from her voice. She had accepted the brush with Hayama's men last night as part of the game and was willing to adapt herself to it. Her courage would undoubtedly prove an asset at a later date.

"I think I can say, without fear of being criticized, that you're the prettiest deck hand we've ever had aboard the *Malacca Maid*. Good nurse, too." He flexed the injured shoulder experimentally and noted with satisfaction that most of the stiffness had disappeared, although it was still a bit tender.

He propped one foot on the hatch and watched her appreciably as she picked up the sail and continued to sew. Her face colored slightly, but her mouth curved in an embarrassed smile at his compliment. The wind caught her hair and whipped the black strands across her face. She brushed it back with one arm and looked up at Darrow. "Did you have any luck today, Captain Darrow? I must say you're in much better spirits than last night."

"It was good to a point. Then it got bad." He was thinking of the connection between the man he had found at Yang She's and Suto Hayama. "We're up against more than we figured on." He hesitated, trying to determine if it was wise to tell her what he had learned.

She would find out sooner or later, he decided, and it was best that she know from the start what they were getting into.

Without going too much into detail, he told her of what he had found and what he knew of the operations of Suto Hayama. "In my opinion, he's as dangerous as any man in Macao. He'll stop at nothing to get what he wants. I remember one time last year he had a waiter killed because the boy spilled a drink in his lap. Somehow or other, he gets away with it all. I don't think he's been inside a jail in his life. Somewhere, higher up, someone's knocking down a pretty penny for keeping the authorities off his neck."

He stopped briefly and lighted a cigarette. "He's not alone in this though. You said last night that only two people in the world knew of the cargo on the *Mary Owen*. Who might the other person be?"

"Maybe I was jumping to conclusions when I said that. I was referring to myself and General Chang Tse Tung. But then I'm not even sure he survived the wreck. Someone has found out about it and when I tried to reason it out, his name was the only one that made sense. My father swore he had never mentioned it to a soul." She put the sailcloth down again and walked to the rail. "You know as much about it as I do now, Captain Darrow."

The sun was beating down unmercifully out of a cloudless sky and even the breeze was hot. Darrow wiped the sweat from his face with the back of his arm and stared across the harbor at Suto Hayama's pier. It was about a half mile away from the *Malacca Maid* and two of the three junks were rolling at anchor. Hayama owned a good stretch of waterfront and for that reason, there was no other shipping docked within the immediate area. The setup was perfect for what he had in mind.

He studied the junks closely and was disappointed to find that the faster of the three was not there. The only one that might possibly be able to outrun him. Darrow decided to settle for what he could get. He'd have to worry about the other one when the time came. At least Hayama would find out that he was playing with fire.

"Come on, let's have a drink." He took Elizabeth's arm and led her to his cabin.

The large, overhead fan made the compartment only slightly cooler than the outside air, but at least they were out of the sun. Elizabeth seated herself on the bunk and watched him curiously as he mixed the drinks. "You're a strange man, Captain Darrow. Your First Mate has been telling me all about you." She blew a strand of hair out of her eyes and settled back against the bulkhead.

"Bart Adams doesn't know when to keep his mouth shut. My life is my own and I, for one, am quite happy with it." He brought her drink and settled in the chair against the opposite bulkhead. "I suppose the next thing you'll ask me is why I never got married and settled down to raising a family in the States."

She smiled at that. "You not only know the sea, Captain, but you're a pretty good judge of the female mind. I'll pass that question if you like. How long have you been Captain of the *Malacca Maid*?"

Darrow sipped his drink and stared at it thoughtfully before answering. He never had been one for small talk and at this time, he felt even less like it than usual. "You ask a lot of questions, Miss McClain."

"I'm sorry if I seem to be prying. I didn't mean to really. Just making conversation. Forget it." Her tongue flicked out and licked at her lips and she swung one foot idly back and forth.

He laughed. She was like a hundred other women he had known. More beautiful perhaps and more poised, but basically, way down deep, they were all the same. "I'm sorry. I didn't mean to be rude. It's no secret, I've had the *Malacca Maid* for ten years now.

In 1945, I was a twenty-four-year-old Lieutenant J.G. on a submarine. Bart Adams was our Chief Bos'n Mate. We were on patrol one night off the China coast and we hit a mine. Bart and I spent six months in China hiding from the Japs. I learned to love the Orient during those months."

He paused and leaning back in the chair, closed his eyes. "My father owned a pineapple plantation in the Hawaiian Islands. The *Malacca Maid* was his pride and joy, but when the war ended, I managed to talk him out of her. Adams came with me and we've been here ever since."

Darrow opened his eyes again and sat upright in the chair. He tipped the glass to his lips and drained it. "Interview's over, Miss McClain. I have a job to do tonight and I need some sleep." He stepped to the hatch and slid it open.

She set her drink down and stepped through the door. "Thanks for the talk, Captain. I just want to say that I ... well, I think I'm in pretty good hands." She climbed the stairwell gracefully, leaving Darrow staring up after her. When she disappeared onto the deck, he remained there, looking up at the empty space she had filled so well.

He stretched out on the bunk presently and closed his eyes in an effort to sleep, but sleep wouldn't come. He suddenly remembered he hadn't had a solid meal in twenty-four hours and, swinging back out of the bunk, left his cabin and made his way to the galley.

He returned in an hour or so and stretched out on the bunk again. This time his eyes were heavy and he was asleep as soon as his head hit the pillow.

At midnight, Bart Adams rapped softly on the door. "Rise and shine, skipper. It's twelve o'clock."

Darrow acknowledged the call and listened to the sound of Adams' feet retreating back onto the deck. He stretched the sleep out of his body and swung his feet to the deck. He showered slowly and let the needle-like drops of cold water pepper his skin, at the same time scrubbing methodically with a stiff brush until his body was red.

He swung the injured shoulder a couple of times, working the stiffness out and making certain that the activity wouldn't reopen the wound. Satisfied, he stepped out of the shower and climbed into his shorts without bothering to dry.

Adams was alone when he reached the deck, leaning against the hatch and puffing casually on the much-used pipe. The lights of Macao tinted the night sky with hues of red and yellow and the sounds of activity from the various boats drifted across the water to the *Malacca Maid*. A sailor staggered rather uncertainly down the deck in the direction of town, singing loudly in Portuguese.

"We ready to sail, Bart?"

"That we are, skipper. Fit as we'll ever be. The crew is grabbin' a little fast shut-eye below decks, but they'll be set when you give the word." He eyed Darrow's shorts, curiously. "You trying to beat the heat or are you goin' callin' on our passenger?"

"Don't be funny, Mr. Adams. I'm going to pay a visit on Suto Hayama. We're going after big game when we leave here and I have reason to believe Suto might want to cut in. I might not be able to stop him, but I can take some of the wind out of his sails." He had not as yet revealed the events of the last two days to Adams and now he related them as rapidly as possible.

When Darrow had finished, Adams whistled softly and did his own variation of an Irish jig. "Twelve million bucks and the makin's of a good scrap. Skipper, you've added ten years to my life. I swear to God I was goin' stale as 'last week's bread.' I never did like that Hayama fella, anyway."

"Don't get frisky yet. We're a hell of a long ways from looking at those gold bars and that 'scrap' as you call it with Hayama, might get a little rough. Now here's what I want you to do. We're going to even the odds a bit. Break out the SCUBA gear, fill one set of tanks and check the whole thing over for me. I'm going to make like the Fourth of July."

Darrow pried open one of the crates marked "dry goods" and pulled out twenty-one-pound blocks of TNT. He cut off two ten-foot sections of the time fuse and in a few minutes, he had taped together two deadly packages.

Adams came up from below decks with the SCUBA gear and helped Darrow slip into it,

They checked their watches. It was a quarter after one. "All right, Bart, here's what to do. Roll out Apiki and O'Mally and get ready to sail. In twenty-five minutes cast off. In thirty-five minutes pick me up by the marker buoy at the head of the channel. Keep your running lights out until after I come back aboard. Any questions?"

"What if you're not there? That doesn't give you much time."

"I'll be there. Just make sure that you are."

They shook hands silently and Darrow slipped over the side, the explosives fastened to his belt. The water was cold as compared to the heat of the night air and he gasped as the chill hit him. He made a last-minute check of the breathing apparatus and kicked away from the ship, diving to about ten feet below the surface. It would be slower under water, but he could afford to take no chances on being spotted by anyone on the junks.

CHAPTER SIX

The harbor was calm and he made good time. Much better than he had expected. As he swam, he could visualize the cruel face of Suto Hayama. The black eyes that never stopped shifting in their sunken sockets. The scar from an old knife wound that ran from the edge of the thin-lipped mouth to the right ear. He would have given a lot to see that face when the junks went up.

In the past years, he and Hayama had let each other alone out of mutual respect of the other's abilities. Now Hayama had crossed the line and there would be no turning back for either of them. One, or possibly both, would die before it was over.

Darrow surfaced shortly and the dimly lit outlines of the two junks loomed in the darkness a hundred feet ahead. The farthest one appeared deserted, but on the deck of the other, two men leaned against the rail and looked out over the water in Darrow's direction. As he watched, one lighted a cigarette, then flipped the burning match over the side. The sound of their lowered voices drifted across the water, but he could make nothing of the conversation.

He had spit the breathing tube from his mouth and now he adjusted it again and allowed himself to slip silently below the surface. The next time he came up, he was between the two ships and he broke water only long enough to scan the decks on each side. They appeared to be empty. He attached the charge to the hull of the first junk two feet below the water line. The time fuse would burn at the rate of a foot a minute, giving him plenty of time to clear the area. He wouldn't want to be anywhere around when these babies went up.

It was then he thought of the men on the ships. Could he slaughter them in cold blood? They were scum to be sure. Murderers, thieves. Men that would not think twice about cutting his throat while he slept. "The hell with it!" he thought. He would have to figure a way to draw them out of the ships. He attached the second charge and then ignited them both.

He swam swiftly for a hundred feet along the pier, searched for a ladder, found it and climbed out of the water. He slipped once and the metal oxygen tanks clanged noisily against the steel ladder. He swore viciously at his clumsiness and hugged the pier, his ears straining to catch any sound that would indicate he had been heard.

There was none and he rose and crossed the pier slowly, his flippers slapping against the rough boards.

He reached the shadows of a warehouse and melted

into them with a sigh of relief. He checked his watch. Six minutes before the charges went off. He looked around cautiously, racking his brain for a way to draw the men from the ships.

Then he found it. The answer was right under his nose. A fifty-gallon fuel drum stood against the of side the building.

He rocked it gently and listened to the gasoline splash around within. It was about half full.

The bung was loose and he unscrewed it easily with his hand, letting the air rush in with a sucking sound. He grabbed it by the rim and, putting his weight behind it, began to tip it slowly to one side. The gasoline sloshed too quickly to the downward side of the drum and Darrow lost his grip, letting it fall with a reverberating rumble that echoed up and down the pier. "Damn it to hell!" The gas spilled out of the uncapped bung hole and splattered over the wooden planking.

A light went on in the next building and from the junks, a man yelled something in Chinese. Darrow checked his watch. Four minutes to go for the blast. He backed off and struck a match against the side of the building. He let it burn for a second until it reached its peak and then pitched it into the pool of gasoline.

A door behind Darrow swung open unexpectedly and two men shot out. He hadn't planned on guards, but he should have known. He caught the first one flush on the jaw with a full swing of his fist and the man dropped like a sack of wheat. The second man was on him before he could regain his balance and they tumbled hard to the planking. The hard rim of his oxygen tanks dug into Darrow's back and the man had one elbow under his throat cutting off his wind. He brought his knee up hard and the fellow doubled up and rolled to one side.

By the time he regained his feet, the dock in the direction of the junks was crawling with men. He'd gotten them out of the boats all right, but he wasn't too happy about it now. A quick series of shots barked out from the onrushing men and he could hear the high-pitched whine of bullets whistling past him.

He made a dash for the end of the pier, but tripped on his flippers and fell hard to the planks. They were all around him before he could move and when he attempted to rise, a foot lashed out and caught him on the side on the head.

He got up slowly this time and found himself looking down the barrel of a .45. He recognized the man behind it as Pedro Sanches, the Captain of one of Hayama's junks.

Sanches screamed excitedly at the men around him. "Put out that damn fire! I'll take care of this bastard. Put out the damn fire!" He glared at Darrow, his eyes wild in the flickering light of the flames.

"You son of a bitch, Darrow. I've waited a long time for this. When Suto gets through with you, you'll wish you'd never been born." He motioned with the .45. "Start walking for the boat and I hope to hell you try something."

Darrow glanced quickly at his watch. Two minutes to go. He had to stall or he'd be flapping through the air with the seas gulls when that TNT went off. "O.K., Sanches, O.K. So you caught me. No need to get sore about it. It's not your building that's burning. You're just another of Hayama's poor stupid boot lickers that cowers in a corner every time he raises an eyebrow."

The .45 flashed through the air and Darrow felt the bones crunch in his nose when it landed. This is a hell of a hard way to gain time, he thought. He was flat on his back and he could feel the rough splinters of the pier grinding into his elbows. The blood was rushing from his nose into the back of his throat and was choking him. He rolled to one side and spit.

Sanches landed a foot hard in Darrow's mid-section and waved the .45 again. "Get up, you bastard! Get up or I'll kill you."

Darrow took the hint. He knew Sanches would like nothing better. He got slowly to his knees, clutching his stomach with both hands. He sucked air into his deflated lungs and climbed the rest of the way to his feet. He looked at his watch again, but his vision was cloudy and he couldn't see the hands. Sanches prodded him hard in the back and he lurched forward unsteadily, edging closer to the edge of the pier.

He glanced over his shoulder and behind him the flames licked hungrily at the sides of the warehouse. Suddenly he realized that the fuel drum would pop any second, too. He quickened his stride and edged still nearer the water. The junks were sitting quietly at anchor only fifty feet away now.

The gasoline drum went up with a roar and Darrow made his move, hoping that the explosion would throw Sanches off for just a second. He hit the water on the flat of his stomach and the face mask that he had pushed up on his forehead was ripped away.

He kicked hard for the bottom and searched frantically for his oxygen tube. He found it, shoved it into place and swallowed a mouthful of sea water in doing so.

The oxygen restored some of his expended energy and he put on an added burst of speed. The blood was still flowing into his throat from the broken nose, however, and before long, he was choking. He had to surface.

When he broke water, he was about two hundred yards from the pier. Sanches and two others were standing on the edge and when they saw him, one man cut loose with a tommy gun. Darrow could see the white spouts as the first slugs hit the water twenty feet away and began to work nearer. He was powerless. His exhausted lungs were gasping wildly for air and instead were sucking in blood, then coughing it out again. A ripple of lead chopped at the water near his side and he knew he was as good as dead. Then the junks went up.

There was the deafening roar first, then the billowing flame that rolled down the pier and engulfed the three men as he watched. The concussion lifted him half way out of the water, then dropped him back. His insides felt as though they were going to burst through his hide. He was swallowing more salt water. Salt water and blood. He struggled to reach the surface again and then rolled on his back, fighting to regain his breath. He cleared his throat the best he could and took the air tube between his teeth.

He looked at his watch. The crystal was shattered. He rolled back onto his stomach and struck out weakly for the rendezvous point. He'd never make it. He was sure he'd never make it.

He barely realized that Bart Adams and Elizabeth McClain were pulling his spent body over the rail of the *Malacca Maid*. He collapsed to the deck and the steady drone of the engines vibrated through his whole body. They were underway. Then he passed out.

CHAPTER SEVEN

When he awoke, he lay there for a long time, staring at the bottom of the bunk above him. The effects of two beatings in the last twenty-four hours had taken their toll and it would have been easy, damned easy, to roll back on his side and wash his hands of the whole rotten mess.

He reached up wearily and ran his fingers over the latest casualty, his broken nose. From the way it felt, it could have covered half his face. The only way it was possible to breathe was through his mouth and with the clotted blood and saliva, that was no cinch.

He turned his head carefully and surveyed the cabin. A small light burning softly in the washroom, sprayed through the partly open door and dimly illuminated the compartment. He was alone.

He realized suddenly that he was going to be sick. He eased over the side of the bunk and on unsteady legs, made a dash for the head. When he was through, he felt better. He turned on the cold water tap in the basin and stuck his head under it groggily. After that, he opened the liquor cabinet and filled a water glass with scotch. The first mouthful he swished around gently, gargled briefly, and spit into the wash basin. There was about three quarters of the drink left and he downed it without lowering the glass.

The warm glow of the liquor spread slowly through his body, creeping into the stomach, the cells, the blood and finally caressing the brain with a soft massage that erased the dull aches that plagued his body. The tired feeling was still there, though. His leg and shoulder muscles had knotted painfully from the swim and after the drink, he wanted more than ever to crawl back into the bunk and sleep away the rest of the cruise.

That was out of the question, however, and he forced himself to slide open the door, move down the corridor, and climb the few short steps to the deck. He walked to the rail without looking to either side and leaned against it weakly, letting the refreshing coolness of the ocean spray bathe his face and bare shoulders and legs.

The *Malacca Maid* was cutting gracefully through the gentle swells and for the first time, Darrow realized that the engines had been cut. He raised his eyes to see the sails billowing fully in the stiff breeze overhead, the moon darted flirtatiously in and out of the black clouds that spotted the heavens. Across the water, the whitecaps glistened whitely in the light of the moon and past that, several miles away, the dim lights of the offshore islands twinkled in the darkness.

He caressed his nose with the fingers of his right hand and he thought of Pedro Sanches. Darrow hoped that he hadn't been killed when the junks blew up, because he had a personal score to settle with Sanches. If the man was still alive, they would meet some day and when they did, Darrow would do a little bone breaking of his own. It would be a long time before he forgot the look in Sanches' eyes as he lashed out with the .45.

Darrow turned at the sound of a voice to find Elizabeth standing at his side. He was surprised to find another person standing behind her. Someone he didn't recognize.

"You remember my uncle, Captain Darrow ... Peter Vargas." She extended her arm and placed a hand on Darrow's wrist.

Darrow recognized the man before she spoke the name. "Vargas!" What the hell! He swore softly.

"How are you, Captain?" He stuck out his hand and took Darrow's in a half-hearted handshake. "I'm sorry I wasn't able to consult you before coming aboard. I was delayed until the last minute. As a matter of fact, your ship was preparing to put to sea when I got here. I managed to persuade Mr. Adams to let me remain, however." Vargas was of American birth, but after years in Singapore, his speech had taken on a slight British accent.

Darrow withdrew his hand with the strange feeling that he had just been handling a dead fish. That was all the expression Vargas had put into the greeting. He realized suddenly that he didn't like the man. He didn't know why. Just a feeling he couldn't shake. He decided that, out of respect for Elizabeth, it would be best to conceal his true feelings of hostility.

"Well, you're aboard. No harm done, I suppose." He

looked at Elizabeth curiously.

Vargas interpreted the look and said, "Elizabeth didn't know I was planning to accompany her. Neither did I, until the last minute for that matter. With twelve million dollars involved, however, I felt she should have someone along to protect her interests." He hooked an arm in a fatherly fashion around her shoulders. "After all, now that my poor brother-in-law has passed on, I'm the only person she has to look after her." Darrow reflected that, in his own mind, she would have been better off alone. He looked at Elizabeth and the light of the moon showed the displeasure in his face. "You didn't tell me that you had told Vargas about the twelve million dollars."

Elizabeth was angered at the tone of the question. "I didn't think that was any of your business, Captain. Of course, I told him. He's my Mother's brother and I saw no reason why I shouldn't have. I told you he was the one that had recommended you for the job."

She was peeved now and Darrow decided to drop it for the time being. He should have guessed that she would tell Vargas the whole story. There was still a deep feeling of distrust, but Darrow brushed it aside as having no foundation. There was no reason he knew of why he shouldn't trust the man.

Vargas pulled a cigar from the pocket of his white suit coat and lit it carefully. Darrow studied his face briefly in the flickering light of the match. He was dark complected, as was Elizabeth, in his late forties, a little overweight perhaps, but still in good shape for his age. His hairline was receding a good bit back from his forehead and his nose was large, arching slightly in the center. The lips were thick and formed in a constant grin that gave one the impression that he was sneering disdainfully at the world. Darrow cursed his habit of forming quick impressions and pushed the matter from his mind.

Elizabeth removed her hand from Darrow's wrist. "I hope you're not angry, Captain. I don't see ..."

"Why should I be angry, Miss McClain?" Darrow cut in sharply. "You chartered the ship. Bring aboard all you like. In the future, I wish you would tell me so I can stock the ship's stores for them, that's all."

"I told you she didn't know about it, Darrow," Vargas said acidly. "If it's the possibility of splitting the gold another way that bothers you, forget it. You obviously want the gold much more than I do and, besides, Elizabeth has already offered me a good portion of her share and I refused. I have more than enough money to last me for the rest of my life."

Darrow was mad now and he wanted to reach out and flatten that hook nose of Vargas'. He was mad at himself, too, because he wasn't at all sure that Vargas hadn't hit close to the truth. There was a little greed in every man and he supposed that he was no exception. Subconsciously, that may have been the reason for his sudden dislike of the man. "I'll forget you said that, Vargas. I think perhaps you had better forget it too."

"I'm sorry. You're right. We've both been hasty." He took Elizabeth's hand in his own and patted it gently. "Come, my dear, I'll see you to your cabin. It has been an exciting night for all of us and we'll feel better, I'm sure, with a little rest."

Darrow watched them as they left the deck and went below. He had no right to act that way and he knew it. He didn't know why he had popped off like that. Was it greed? After thirty-four years, was John Darrow getting money hungry all of a sudden? He'd never given a damn about it before. "Ah, hell!" There was a bitter taste in his mouth and he spit angrily over the side.

He lighted a cigarette and walked slowly to Bart Adams who stood at the helm. "How we doing, Bart?" He checked the compass and found it to be on the proper course of 310 degrees.

"Moving right along, Skipper. How you feelin'?"

"I've felt better in my day, but I guess I'll make it. What time do you have?" The salt spray had extinguished his cigarette and he flipped it over the side, still mad at himself.

Adams replied without looking at his watch. "About 3:45. Should be getting light before long." He leaned easily on the wheel, dividing his gaze between the compass needle and what he could see of the water ahead. "Pretty good show you put on with Hayama tonight. We were afraid for a while you weren't going to make it."

"I was a little concerned about that myself." His eyes searched the ocean behind them. The fluorescent wake of the *Malacca Maid* stretched out for several hundred feet astern, being eventually absorbed by the darkness of the night. Aside from that, there was nothing. "I was rather surprised to find that we had a new passenger."

Adams wiped the ocean spray from his face with

the back of his sleeve. "I kind o' thought you would be. Struck me as funny, too." He stopped for a minute as if trying to decide if his thoughts were important enough to pass on. "We no sooner started the engines than this fella comes up from out o' nowhere and hops aboard. Just like that. I'd been watching the dock as much as I could, but I never saw him approach. Almost like he was hiding there, waitin' for us to pull out. Well, anyway, he was aboard and I didn't have time to argue. Miss McClain was as surprised as any of us from the way she acted, but him bein' her uncle and all, I decided to let him stay." He checked the compass and finding them a bit off course, moved the wheel to adjust. "If I made the wrong decision, I guess it's a little late to correct it now." He nodded his head in the direction of the offshore islands. "That's quite a swim."

"I would most likely have done the same thing, Bart. Let's keep an eye on this bird, though. I'm not sure I fully trust him."

Adams nodded his agreement and Darrow moved off in the direction of the bow, checking the rigging with an experienced eye as he walked. It was good to be at sea again, to feel the rise and fall of the deck beneath his feet, the salt spray blowing against his skin and to hear the flapping of the canvas as a good stiff wind buffeted the sails.

He remembered for the first time that he was still in his shorts and he thought of standing there, talking with Elizabeth, only a few minutes ago. He laughed aloud and the sound of his voice was strange in the stillness of the night. "If she hasn't seen a man in his shorts before, it's sure as hell about time."

CHAPTER EIGHT

"Did you say something, Captain Darrow?" He hadn't seen Elizabeth sitting on the deck with her back against the forward hatch.

At first, he was flustered. Afraid that she might have heard. But when she gave no sign, he regained his composure and seated himself on the hatch above her. "No, nothing important. I was just talking to the ship. You think that's strange, I suppose." He was lying, but he thought the answer was good.

"No, not really. I suppose when a man spends as much time at sea as you have, he has to talk to something. I know my father used to do it. He used to tell me that during the war he'd be standing watch at night and he got so he would carry on long conversations with his ship. I guess you come to regard them as you would a woman after a while. Is that right?"

"I guess that's so. I thought you had turned in. What's the matter, can't you sleep?" He couldn't figure her out. Ten minutes ago she'd been angry at his reaction to seeing Vargas. Now she was sitting there talking like nothing had happened. Sometimes, he wondered if he would ever understand women.

"It was too hot to sleep. After Uncle Peter went to his cabin, I decided to come back up for a breath of air. It really is wonderful up here. I can see why men love the sea. I think I could learn to love it too."

Darrow slid off the hatch and relaxed on the deck at

her side. "The sun's about to come up." He said nothing more, but watched the east expectantly and as he looked, the first flash of grey appeared on the horizon, growing steadily until it covered a good half of the sky. Then, as it always did, the red ball of the sun peeked over the rim of the sea and cast a blood red tint upon the waters. Darrow always made a point of being on deck at this time and every morning he watched the sky as he was now. When he tired of that, he'd leave the sea. You could give them their forests, their rivers, their lakes, their tall buildings, their flowing fields or their towering mountains.

Give them what they chose and he'd pit this sight against it any day.

Suddenly he was aware of Elizabeth's closeness. He watched her out of the corner of his eyes and he was struck with a sudden desire to grab her and smother her in his arms. Her white shorts were wrinkled up tightly against the lower part of her body and the loose-fitting blouse had been whipped aside by the wind, exposing a generous portion of her rounded breasts. He pried his eyes away from her with an effort. He would have to watch himself. He would have to remember that this was a business partnership and nothing more. He had made it a policy in the past never to mix business with pleasure and it had kept him out of trouble on several occasions. He wouldn't want to change now, no matter how hard it might be.

"You have taken quite a beating in the last two days, Captain. Why don't you let me dress your shoulder and then see if I can't get some of that swelling out of your nose?" She looked at him and there was tenderness in her eyes. "I think a lot of lesser men would have backed out by this time."

He turned the suggestion over in his mind for a second and decided that it was one worthy of action. He couldn't take a chance now of getting an infection in that knife wound. He smiled gratefully and nodded his head in agreement. "All right. Let me shower real fast. Come on down in five or ten minutes." He got stiffly to his feet. "Thanks for the concern."

He turned and made his way back to his cabin. He shaved quickly and stepped into an ice-cold shower, lingering under the refreshing coolness of the needle-sharp spray. He soaped down vigorously after a few minutes and then rinsed himself. He shut off the water and stepped out of the stall slowly, wishing he could stay there all morning.

He had folded a fresh pair of white ducks over the towel rack and he slipped into them after drying himself quickly. When he stepped out of the head, Elizabeth was already in the cabin. She had seated herself comfortably on his bunk and was leaning back against the bulkhead with her eyes closed, a gentle, dreamy expression on her beautiful face.

"You can open your eyes," he said. "I'm decent." He sat on the bunk beside her.

She looked in awe at the wicked gash in his shoulder. It was starting to heal well, but the wound was still puffed and jagged and the flesh around it was red and swollen. When she spoke, however, her voice was firm and confident. "Lie down on the bunk and let me look at it." She rose and, taking his arm, guided him dominantly to a prone position on the cot.

She stepped to the medicine cabinet and returned with a variety of bottles, cotton swabs, bandage and adhesive.

Darrow winced as she dug at the wound with the first swab, cleansing it thoroughly with peroxide. When she satisfied herself that it was sterile, she took a second swab and smeared it with iodine. "It doesn't seem to be infected."

"It isn't as bad as it looks, I don't think. The damn thing never has bothered me much. Just a little stiffness now and then." He was watching her face as she worked and again he had to fight down a desire to take her in his arms.

When she finished with the bandaging, she ran cold water over a wash rag and began to bathe the swollen nose.

Her blouse was still parted slightly at the top and Darrow could see that she was wearing no brassiere. Her thigh rested easily against Darrow's side and the urge to grab her was suddenly overpowering. He decided to let the past policy of not mixing business and pleasure go to hell and before she could object, his arm had encircled her neck and he pulled her down on top of him.

She struggled at first, fiercely, tiger-like. Her hands clawed at his arms and he could see the fire in her dark eyes. Their lips came together, she tried to say something, but couldn't. Then she relaxed and her arms clutched at his shoulders. She wasn't fighting anymore.

She moaned softly, continually. Her lithe body undulated rhythmically against him, one hand crept to his scalp and her fingers tugged at his close-cropped hair. Her lips returned his kiss violently and her tongue darted swiftly, passionately, in and out between his teeth.

Darrow, hands trembling, worked clumsily at the buttons on her blouse. It fell away finally, revealing in startling contrast, the snowy whiteness of her heaving breasts against the bronzed skin that had been exposed to the sun. When he fumbled unsuccessfully with the zipper on her shorts, she moved away quickly and slipped out of them herself.

She stood there, naked, before him. Almost defiantly, she smiled.

He liked that. So she has the defiance of the northern blood, too, he thought. He had already noticed the deep passion of the Mediterranean in her, and yet the quiet, submissive wisdom so reminiscent of the Orient. Now—the white-hot turbulence of the Cossacks— what a prize!

He reached out for the proud, full breasts of snow, tipped blood-red at the ends. They turned to molten mounds of desire under his strong hands, their tips hard, small rocks of pulsating desire. She moved toward him, almost instinctively, until her flat bronzed tummy met the hard stubble of his masculine chin. She swayed against it, like a ship against the wind, moaning louder, deeper in her throat, her body doing things it had never dreamed of doing before. And Darrow played her like a ship, cruelly but gently, anticipating her every whim, navigating her expertly through undreamed of whirlpools into the sun itself at the tip of the horizon....

When they had finished, neither moved for several minutes. The bunk was small, built for one person, but they made do. Darrow rolled partly on his back and Elizabeth cuddled against him like a contented kitten. "You took advantage of me, John," she said. She wasn't angry though, she was smiling. Her fingers toyed playfully with his lips and his eyebrows.

"I'm sorry. I guess I stepped out of line."

"You needn't be. I think we were destined from the start to come to this!" She hesitated for a moment. "Is it ... is it just one of those things, John, or is it more than that? Do you think of me now as just another of the many girls you must have known before?" Her eyes were troubled.

"I don't know, Elizabeth. I don't know." He answered her truthfully, regretfully. He hadn't intended for it to go this far. Now that it had, he wasn't at all sure what he felt. He was confused, befuddled.

She lifted herself slowly from his side and disappeared into the head. When she came out, she was still smiling, her eyes flashed joyously. "I'm glad you said that. Believe it or not I'm glad. I wouldn't have wanted you to lie to me. I ... I'm not sure how I feel either. It may be just a physical attraction. It may be more. Time will tell." She walked to the bunk and kissed him, then slid open the door and disappeared into the passageway.

CHAPTER NINE

When she had gone, Darrow dressed slowly, methodically, then made his way to the galley. A pot of coffee was in its usual place on the stove and he poured a cup, sipping it gingerly as it seared his lips. Surprisingly enough, he wasn't tired any longer. The session with Elizabeth had served to stimulate him rather than tire him. He seemed to have his second wind now and he knew that he could go on for many hours yet. He hated to count the scant moments of sleep he had had in the last two days. He laughed harshly. What little sleep he did have had come as a result of being beaten into it.

He finished the coffee and climbed out on deck. With his binoculars, he swept the horizon to their rear, but there was no sign of Hayama. He was back there though. He was out of sight, but Darrow could feel his presence. It was a sixth sense that he had always had. One that had proven itself in the past. They would have to be prepared for the worst.

He broke out the Browning Automatic Rifle and stripped it down, changing the gummy Cosmoline for a light coat of oil. He loaded the ten magazines that were packed with it and then mounted it on top of the cabin. He set a box of five hundred rounds of extra ammunition beside it, then covered the whole thing with a tarp and tied it down. This wouldn't match the fire power of Hayama's junk, but it was a hell of a lot better than nothing.

Apiki had relieved Adams at the wheel and O'Mally was on the stern working over the compressor.

Adams stepped to Darrow's side and pulled the much-used pipe from his pocket. Dark shadows of fatigue circled his eyes and his voice was heavy. "You think we lost 'em skipper?"

"I doubt it." He struck a match and held it for his first mate. "Hayama isn't one to give up this easy. He's back there and he's mad. Mad as a wet hen. He'll find us before the day is over, I'm sure of it."

Adams took the match from Darrow and held it over the pipe, cupping his hand to protect the flame from the wind "You don't think that BAR is going to be a match for him do you? That's like a man hunting tigers with a fly swatter."

Darrow smiled, half-heartedly. "I'm not hunting him, Bart. You're right though, I wish we had a cannon, but we don't. We'll just have to make the best of what we have." He turned and, folding his arms on the cabin top, stared absently at the horizon to the rear.

Adams nodded and said nothing. What was there to say? They would meet Hayama, there would be a fight and the outcome, if it was in their favor, would be by the grace of "lady luck." They had been in tough spots before and come out of it all right. It would be bad luck to believe that it was going to be any different this time.

Darrow lighted a cigarette and stuck the charred match in the cellophane wrapper around the cigarettes. "Why don't you get some sleep, Bart. When things die down a bit, I'll probably fold up like a busted mizzen mast and you won't be able to wake me for a week. When that happens, I'll need a clearheaded First Mate to take command."

Adams agreed. "You're right there. I think I'll have a quick bit to eat and sack out. See you later, Skipper." He lifted his hand wearily in a mock salute and disappeared through the hatch.

Darrow remained in the same position for the next thirty minutes, moving only to sweep the horizon with his binoculars every now and then. Finally, he let the glasses fall to his chest at the end of their strap and stepped through the hatch.

Elizabeth was in the galley when he entered and the pleasant aroma of perking coffee filled his nostrils. He rubbed his hands together briskly and grinned at her. "You must be psychic. I've been thinking about fresh coffee for the last ten minutes." He thought it best to make no mention of what had transpired earlier and evidently she felt the same, for she said nothing and gave no sign that anything was different.

"I'm not really. I guess I'm just another coffee hound. I could live on the darned stuff. Sometimes, I get so I can't think unless I have a steaming cup in front of me." She lifted two mugs from their hooks about the stove and set them on the table. She sniffed experimentally over the coffee pot and, deciding it was about ready, turned off the flame and filled the cups.

Darrow took one of the mugs and lifted it thirstily to his lips, then lowered it hurriedly, swearing softly as the hot liquid burned his tongue.

Elizabeth laughed at his startled look. "That stuff is hot when it boils, or didn't you know?" She blew the steam away from her own cup.

He smiled, partly at her and partly at his own stupidity. "Well, now I know what it takes to make you laugh. All I have to do is burn all the hide off my lips and blister my tongue. I'd hate to think what it would take to put you in hysterics."

"I'm sorry." She laughed again. "Sometimes my sense of humor is a little off base. It was funny, though. You looked so flabbergasted."

Elizabeth's teeth showed a glistening white through the curve of her red lips and Darrow studied her pleasant features appreciatively. She was obviously tired, but through the fatigue, a certain freshness was still apparent. It was a freshness of spirit, of mind; he wasn't sure which.

She had lapsed into a thoughtful silence and was staring absently at the mahogany paneling on the bulkheads.

"A penny for your thoughts," he said. "No, wait, don't tell me, I know. You're on a mental shopping spree in San Francisco. We're almost a thousand miles and God knows how many fathoms from the gold and I'll bet in your mind, it's half spent already. How does that Christmas rhyme go? Visions of sugar plums ...?"

"You're right as usual, John. I was climbing aboard the Powell Street cable car and my arms were so loaded down with packages I could hardly make it. The sun was sparkling off of the diamonds that covered my arms and, of course, I was cloaked in fur." She giggled happily.

"If you're going to dream, why don't you go all the way. Look at it like this .... You're coming out of I.

Magnin's. Behind you, a string of servants, four or five at least, are carrying your packages. You walk to the curb and a black limousine pulls up in front of you. The chauffeur steps out smartly and bows as he opens the door." Darrow bowed mockingly as he spoke. "You climb in and settle back. The weather is perfect, but you're troubled. You have a big decision to make. Should you go on to your San Francisco mansion, your modest little fifty-thousand-dollar beach house at Carmel, or do you need a change? Should you charter a plane and fly to your villa on the Riviera? Finally, you make up your mind and your chauffeur speeds off to the International Airport. You're going to the Riviera." Darrow finished with a flourishing sweep of his arms, grinning foolishly at his own humor.

Elizabeth laughed and sipped loudly on the coffee. "Boy! I thought I was a dreamer. You really dream in style, though, don't you!"

"Not usually," he chuckled. "No, I guess you'd call me pretty much of a realist. I was just making a poor attempt at being a comedian."

Elizabeth smiled and there was silence for a moment while each was absorbed in his own thoughts. Then the door opened and Vargas stepped in.

"Good morning, everyone." His voice was bubbling with cheer. "Beautiful morning. I was just out on deck, feel wonderful. Boy, this salt air does something to a man. Lead on to the *Mary Owen*." He stretched and rubbed his chest vigorously with both hands, then walked to the stove and poured a cup of coffee.

Elizabeth acknowledged his greeting cheerfully, but Darrow said nothing. Instead, he finished his coffee and stepped to the door. He was being childish, but what the hell. He just didn't like the man. He stopped half way through the door and twisted around. "Elizabeth, would you do me a favor? Fix up a few eggs and some bacon. I think Mr. Adams has eaten already, but the rest of the crew hasn't. They usually take three or four eggs apiece. I'll relieve Apiki at the helm and then when he eats, I'll be back down." Purposely, he avoided looking at Vargas.

She saluted mockingly. "Aye, aye, sir. You've just signed on a new cook. From now on, leave it up to me. I'll give you bacon and eggs like you never tasted!"

Vargas stepped quickly to Darrow and clutched at his sleeve. "I say, Darrow, isn't there something I can do? I'm not much of a sailor, I grant you, but I hate to feel absolutely useless."

His voice was serious, but Darrow would have bet he was only making a gesture.

Well, he'd asked for it. "O.K., when you finish breakfast, come up on deck and we'll see what we can do. I think we have some lines that need tarring. Better change out of that white suite, though. You're about Adams' size, ask Apiki to get you a set of his denims."

Vargas' face fell ever so slightly and Darrow was grinning as he climbed onto deck. After the lines were freshly tarred, there was always the bilge that needed cleaning.

CHAPTER TEN

He searched the horizon again with the binoculars before relieving Apiki. There was still no sign of Hayama and it puzzled him. The man had had plenty of time to overtake them. What in the hell was he waiting for? He couldn't believe that they had given Hayama the slip. He must have been nearby when Darrow blew up the junks. Even if he was in Hong Kong, the junk was fully equipped with a wireless and radar. It wouldn't have taken long to pick up the trail of the *Malacca Maid*.

Even at night.

Then it hit him. "Radar! Damn it to hell. Why didn't I think of that before?" Darrow spoke aloud, but there was no one on deck to hear him. The answer was obvious. Hayama was sitting back over the horizon, tracking them on his radar. The only question now was, when was he going to strike? Was he going to wait until they started diving in search of the *Mary Owen*, until they raised the gold, if they did, or was he just biding his time? Waiting to strike at the moment they least expected. There was only one thing to do. Wait and see.

The wind was blowing briskly from the northwest, pushing the *Malacca Maid* at a good clip along her course. She was riding high in the water and the salt spray was whipping back over the bow, sweeping her decks. The sun was well up in the morning sky by this time and it was hot where it touched his exposed skin. It was the kind of day Darrow loved.

A half hour later, Apiki came up from the galley and relieved him at the helm. Darrow went below and ate a hearty breakfast, gulping it down hungrily and at the same time feasting his eyes on Elizabeth, who sat silently across from him, drinking coffee. Not only was she beautiful, but she was the best cook that Darrow could remember having aboard the *Maid*. He wished it could have been under different circumstances.

He returned to the deck after breakfast and once more searched the horizon. Still nothing. It was beginning to get on his nerves and from the looks of the others, it was bothering them too. He wished to hell Hayama would get on with it.

O'Mally was still working patiently over the air compressor and after a while, Darrow went forward to give him a hand. "How's she coming, fella? Making any headway?" He knelt beside the compressor and watched.

"Not too bad, Skipper. The damn thing was in pretty rough shape, but I think I'll have her going by the time we have to use her. You want to hand me that wrench over there? I had to replace some of the gears."

Darrow gave him the wrench and then held the shaft, while O'Mally tightened the locking nut into place. The wiring was shot, too, and while the other man worked on the engine itself, Darrow replaced the wiring. It was a long, drawn-out job and by noon they were not even close to being done. It would take another solid day of uninterrupted work before they could even test it.

Peter Vargas had, in the meantime, changed into

working clothes and tackled the much-hated job of tarring line. Darrow paid him no heed, but now and then, distinct sounds of down to earth, four letter swearing could be heard coming from the direction of the tar bucket. With every curse, Darrow's grin became wider and now and then he would break out into an unmuffled chuckle. If Vargas thought this was bad, he should wait until he started cleaning the bilge.

O'Mally eyed Darrow for a while and gathered all the facts in his mind before he spoke. "You don't like that fella Vargas much, do you, Skipper?"

"I don't love the man exactly. I didn't think it showed."

O'Mally nodded and didn't speak for a minute. "I don't care much for the bastard myself. He doesn't know me, but I worked for him one time down in Singapore. Before the war, it was. Never liked him then, either."

Darrow raised his eyebrows in surprise. "I didn't know that. Tell me about it. I'm rather curious about this bird. Never had much to do with him myself."

"Not much to tell," O'Mally kept his voice low. "I worked in one of his warehouses for two years. Then the war came and I joined the British Navy. Vargas stayed behind and to hear him tell it, he spent four years in a Jap prison camp. I heard different, though." O'Mally paused and cleared his throat. "This friend of mine says he was spying for Japan for five or six years before war busted out. My friend is Malayan and he stayed on when the Japs came. Claims Vargas sat out the war on a plush plantation back in the hills. The Japs supplied him with slave labor and he never had it so good. I don't know how true that is, but I have no reason to doubt it. The word came from a good source."

Darrow whistled softly. An interesting biography. The war had been over for ten years and Darrow bore no hard feelings against the Japanese. Nor would he let this information affect his relationship with Vargas. There was one exception to that. The man had been a native born American. He had betrayed the trust of his country. It was more a character trait than anything. The man was not trustworthy.

The rest of the day passed uneventfully. Even swiftly. There was too much work to allow anyone time to concern themselves about a possible meeting with Hayama. It would come, there would be a fight and lives would be lost, but although it was undoubtedly in the back of everyone's mind, no one spoke of it.

Darrow took the two 'til eight watch at the helm and after eating only a light meal, retired to his cabin by nine o'clock. He felt the tiredness immediately when he stretched out on the bunk. His muscles ached, his injured shoulder was throbbing again, his eyes were fogged with strain, and his mind was whirring uncontrollably. Sleep came swiftly, blessedly, like a summer rain to the dying grass.

He woke up automatically at four, dressed and dashed his face with cold water. The heat in the cabin was suffocating and when his chest he reached the deck, he sucked great lungfuls of air into his chest.

The brisk wind that had borne them rapidly over the water for the last twenty-four hours had died somewhat and the dampness hung heavy in the air, mixing with the heat and sapping the strength from men's bodies.

He checked briefly with Adams to find that the night had been uneventful and scanned the horizon with binoculars. After that, he took a fix on the sun and charted the course for that day. The wind had been good. According to his calculations, they had made almost four hundred miles since leaving Macao. Another day and a half similar to the first would put them almost to their destination.

CHAPTER ELEVEN

He was below in the galley and had just finished a hasty breakfast of eggs and potatoes, when the excited cry came from on deck. He barged through the half-opened door, wincing as he banged his injured shoulder on the bulkhead. He took the stairs in three strides and almost collided with Adams who swung down from the top of the cabin.

"We got a junk behind us, Skipper, comin' up fast. I was just on my way to give you the news." He took the pipe from his mouth and knocked the tobacco out of it before jabbing it in his rear pocket.

Darrow climbed to the top of the cabin and took the binoculars from Adams, who had crawled after him. It was Hayama's junk all right. No doubt about that, he would know the lines anywhere. She was a thousand yards astern and closing fast. "How the hell did you let her get so close?"

"I was checkin' regular, Skipper. I checked one time and it was all clear and the next time, there she was.

She must be makin' close to thirty knots."

Darrow checked the situation quickly. Elizabeth and Vargas were on the starboard side, leaning over the rail and staring back excitedly at the oncoming ship. Apiki was at the tiller and O'Mally had climbed the rigging for a better view. The wind had died suddenly and the *Malacca Maid* was making no better than fifteen knots. Hayama had timed it perfectly.

Elizabeth McClain approached the cabin anxiously. "That's Hayama, isn't it? Is he going to catch us?"

"Not if I can help it, he won't. You and your uncle go below."

Vargas moved to Elizabeth's side and Darrow expected to find fear on the man's face. He was rather disappointed to see that it wasn't there. "It looks like we're in for a fight, doesn't it, Darrow. I'd like to help if I can. Just tell me what to do." He was looking at the BAR as Adams stripped the tarp from over it. "I've never used one of those, but I'd like to try."

"I already told Miss McClain what I want you two to do. I'm sending her below and I want you to go along to take care of her in case something happens."

Darrow spun away without giving them a chance to object. "Mr. Adams, take the tiller," Darrow was yelling now. "Apiki, lower the canvas and O'Mally, get those damn engines turning over. If they get much closer, we're dead ducks."

Darrow checked the situation once more as the crew scrambled to their assigned tasks. It was then he noticed the sea. It was smooth as glass and the wind had died to almost nothing. He jumped down from the cabin and checked the barometer quickly. Just as he feared, it had fallen drastically. They were in for a blow. Most likely a bad one. It was the early days of the typhoon season and in this part of the world, they could expect to run into some dillies. The sky confirmed his worst thoughts.

Up to now, he had been almost looking forward to the clash with Hayama. Do it and get it done with. Between the BAR and the power that could be unleashed from the *Malacca Maid*'s twin "Grey Marine" engines, they would have had an excellent chance. Now, with the storm brewing, Darrow realized that even the victor could fall. If they suffered damage that amounted to anything from Hayama's guns, it could place them in a serious predicament if they were forced to ride out a typhoon.

He checked Hayama again and the gap had closed to about seven hundred fifty yards. They would be within firing distance before long. He wondered what in the hell O'Mally was doing down there. The engines should have kicked in long ago. The canvas had been lowered now and they were standing almost still in the water.

Adams was moving about impatiently back of the wheel, swearing blackly and waiting for the engines to start. Now and then he would cast a nervous glance over his shoulder.

Darrow left the barometer and climbed back to the cabin top. He flattened himself behind the BAR and slammed a magazine into place, sighting in on the junk. They were within five hundred yards now and Darrow squeezed the trigger. He could see the men that had been moving around on her decks scatter as he jerked off a short burst. Hayama must not have expected the Malacca Maid to be armed with a weapon of that range for no answering shots rang out and for a moment, there was confusion aboard the junk.

Darrow fired again, this time taking closer aim and someone on her stern slumped to the deck. He shifted the sights to the approximate position of her tiller and the junk veered sharply to port as he squeezed off another short burst.

She was broadside to the *Malacca Maid* now and Darrow raked the decks with the ammunition that remained in the magazine. There was still no answering fire from the junk.

The deck beneath Darrow began to vibrate suddenly as the *Malacca Maid*'s two engines roared to life. The screw turned over in the water, slowly at first, then more rapidly as they began to get under way. The two ships were about eight hundred yards apart now, the junk having lost ground as a result of veering off course. As Darrow watched, it swung back around and fell into line with the wake of the *Malacca Maid*.

On the deck below, Adams had turned the wheel back to Apiki and was jumping around excitedly, waving his arms in a triumphant mockery at the junk.

Darrow picked up the binoculars and studied the junk again. The first element of surprise that had been sprung by the BAR had passed and now Hayama's crew was moving around swiftly, but purposefully. Darrow thought he could pick out Hayama standing beside the man at the tiller, but he wasn't sure.

As Darrow watched, a hatch slid open and two men

popped out, dragging something after them. He wasn't sure and he was half afraid to guess, but it looked a hell of a lot like it might be a fifty-caliber machine gun.

The *Malacca Maid* was under full power now, making perhaps thirty-five knots in the glassy sea. The junk had dropped back to around a thousand yards and Darrow was hopeful that they would be able to outrun her.

Suddenly he knew why they had been gaining ground. Hayama wanted them to and the reason was all too apparent. The foxy son of a bitch had them where he wanted them now. The junk was out of effective range of the BAR, but with a fifty-caliber, he could sit back and pop them off like ducks in a shooting gallery.

Even as Darrow realized this, Hayama's gun cut loose in a sharp, staccato bark and small water spouts appeared in the wake of the Malacca Maid as the fifty began to walk in on them. "Clear the deck! Clear the deck! Adams, take the wheel. The rest of you men, flatten yourselves behind the forward hatch. We're in for it now." He was yelling excitedly, almost frantically and he jammed another magazine into the BAR.

Hayama got the range and the heavy slugs began to tear at the ship. The cabin roof beside Darrow was ripped open with a splintering burst and two more slugs ripped into the deck at the side of the cabin.

The next scattering of shots was higher and part of the main mast was ripped away about half way up. Then they lowered again and he could feel the short shudder as slugs stabbed into the side of the cabin. If they stayed like this, they would be shot to pieces in a matter of minutes. All that was needed was for one slug to find the fuel tanks in the stern, or worse than that, the crates of TNT that were stored below decks.

The rain came suddenly, sweeping in on the first wings of wind from the south. Darrow had to act and act fast. "O'Mally! Get below and reverse the engines. Full speed astern."

Adams yelled wildly. "What the hell you tryin' to do? They're cutting us to pieces now. If we get any closer, we're dead." He released the wheel in his excitement and the *Malacca Maid* rolled heavily back and forth as the tiller spun to one side. Adams grabbed it again and steadied it as Darrow ignored him. Suddenly, he saw the logic in Darrow's actions.

Their only hope was to get closer so that they could go to work with the BAR. Darrow was hoping that by reversing the engines, he could catch the junk off guard and be within range before they realized what was happening.

The *Malacca Maid* shuddered to a halt and the engines vibrated roughly, as they backed water. The distance between the two ships began to close suddenly and the fire from the fifty was going high.

Hayama saw too late what had occurred and by the time he could stop his engines, they were within range of the BAR.

Darrow emptied the magazine at the crew of the fifty-caliber and they scattered for cover. He jerked out the magazine and replaced it with a fresh one, then raked over the tiller. The junk swung hard to port as the wheel went wild. A man scrambled back to the fifty and was cut down with a three-round burst from the BAR.

The magazine was empty again and Darrow slammed another full one home. This time he sprayed the hull of the junk at the water line. The two ships were now only about three hundred yards apart.

A forward hatch of the junk slid open and three men crawled out and blazed away with automatic weapons. They were beginning to recover from the sudden turn of events. Now was the time for Darrow to get out while the getting was good. He turned around on his belly and yelled at Adams. "Reverse engines. Full speed ahead!" He turned back around and scattered another magazine over the deck of the junk. One of the men with the sub machine guns collapsed over the hatch, but the other two continued to fire.

Apiki appeared from below and kneeled at the rail with the *"Malacca Maid"*'s Thompson. He got off one short burst and then collapsed and rolled back on one side, the Thompson limp in his fingers.

The two "Grey Marine" engines were full ahead again and the white wake began to froth behind them as they once more pulled away from the junk. Darrow fired a final burst at the unattended fifty-caliber in an attempt to jam it, but he doubted if he was effective. Then, he crawled down from the cabin top and relieved Adams at the tiller. "Get Apiki below and then check our damage below the water line. Report back as soon as you can."

The rain was coming in sheets now and they were sailing full into the increasing force of the wind. The sea had changed in minutes from its previous glassy face to short, choppy white caps that shook the schooner as she plowed into them. He checked the barometer once again and it had fallen still more.

Darrow couldn't recall seeing a front develop with more suddenness.

He shot a glance back over his shoulder and the junk was about a thousand yards astern, barely visible in the driving rain. Both ships were beginning to pitch and roll heavily in the seas and Darrow felt he could forget about Hayama for the time being. The sea had become too rough for further exchanges of fire.

O'Mally tumbled out of the hatch and grabbed a guy line for support. "I'll take this storm to that machine gun of Hayama's any day. Looks like it's going to be a dandy. Captain." He mumbled something else, but Darrow couldn't hear him above the rising roar of the storm.

He was jolted by a sudden twist of the tiller that almost jerked it from his hands. His muscles strained under his wet shirt as he corrected and headed the bow back into the wind.

O'Mally was still standing braced against the guy line and Darrow remembered the BAR that was still set up atop the cabin. "Take that BAR and ammunition below and reload those empty magazines. You might as well strip it down and start to clean it too. There isn't anything you can do on deck unless something happens. If you see Adams, tell him to shake a leg with that damage report."

O'Mally grunted an, "Aye, aye, sir" and after grabbing the weapon, vanished through the hatch, leaving Darrow alone on deck.

He looked around again to where he had last seen the junk and there was nothing in sight. It had been swallowed up completely by the storm, but that didn't mean it was far away. Visibility had been cut to a hundred feet at the most.

Darrow thought of the holes he had put in their hull with the BAR and he laughed aloud, rather sadistically. That would keep them busy for a while he thought, just pumping water.

CHAPTER TWELVE

A heavy wave broke over their bow and the schooner plowed its nose deep into the sea, came up again bucking, and then shuddered from bow to stern as she dropped back onto the water and took the next wave. The wind had picked up to what Darrow estimated at close to ninety miles an hour and he was having difficulty staying on his feet.

It was then he noticed, for the first time, the mizenmast where the fifty-caliber slug had ripped through, carrying away half the thickness of the wood. If that snapped, it could raise hell with whomever was at the helm, possibly even wreck the tiller itself. Then they would be in for it. A ship without control in these seas, might as well be abandoned.

He picked up the intercom phone and whistled into it. "Mr. Adams, to the helm." Then, as an afterthought, "Mr. Adams and O'Mally, both to the helm." He repeated the order and then dropped the phone, leaving it dangle by the wire as the wheel was ripped from his grasp by a particularly violent wave.

The wheel spun so savagely that it was impossible to stop until it did so of its own accord and by that time, they were broadside to the storm. Another mass of water hit them and broke completely over the ship.

Darrow felt his grip loosen on the wheel and he was being swept along the deck, toward the rail. He reached out frantically, clutching at anything he could find. He grabbed futilely at the deck, as he was washed further along and his fingernails dug into the planking and broke. He felt the hard metal post that supported the rail at his back and he reached out and gripped it with the hold of a man who knows he is fighting death.

He was in the water now as the schooner keeled almost completely to its side and then he was lifted free as she came back up. He crawled halfway back to the tiller, coughing the salt water from his lungs. Another wave hit them and he seized the railing that bordered the helm on three sides. The water swept over him again and once more he lost his hold and was swept toward the sea. He tried again and this time managed to reach the helm, grasping the wheel with all his remaining strength. He twisted hard to port and the bow of the *Malacca Maid* gradually came around.

By the time Adams and O'Mally reached the deck, the tiller was once more under control and their nose was pointed dead into the wind. Adams yelled something in his ear, but it was impossible to hear above the roar of the storm and Darrow motioned for him to take the tiller.

They would have to tie down the mizzenmast before

it snapped completely. The last wave that they took broadside had split it from the bullet damaged center all the way to the base, and it was ready to go at any minute from the way it looked.

Darrow reached inside the hatch and came out with a coil of one inch line. He tried to outshout the storm, but it was no use. He finally got across to O'Mally the nature of their trouble by a series of violent hand signals and the two of them worked their way toward the mast.

It took a good minute of careful groping to move the ten feet and finally, they stopped at the base, looking up at the damage fifteen feet above the deck. It was another hour of work before the mast was tied down and the two men worked their way back to the helm.

The storm still had not abated. If anything, it was worse. The sea was leaping skyward in great white mountains, as if seeking to escape from the terror and fury of the typhoon, but the mighty ocean was as helpless as the feeble creature that called himself "man" and the wind whipped the crest from the mountains, mixed it wildly with the rain and hurled it with a force that only nature can muster against the plunging, writhing, *Malacca Maid*.

Adams turned over the tiller to O'Mally and went below with Darrow.

They closed the hatch behind them and for the first time in two hours, the roar of the storm lessened in Darrow's ears. "How bad is Apiki?"

"He'll be all right, I think." They went to Darrow's cabin and Adams pulled a towel from the head and dried himself.

"Miss McClain is taking care of him in her room. It's just a scalp wound, maybe a slight concussion, too." He passed the towel to Darrow.

The schooner's bow would rise out of the water and fall back with a force that shuddered all forty-eight feet of her. Darrow listened carefully to the creaking of the hull as she strained. "I think she'll pull us through, Bart. If she didn't go down when I let her slip broadside to the storm, she never will. How did you make out on the damage inspection?"

"We have a couple of holes in the hull right at the water line." He pulled the pipe from his pocket, shook the water from it and attempted to fill it. "I patched them up as best I could, but not before we shipped water. We had about a foot in the after hold, so I started the pumps." He finished filling the pipe and leaned against the bulkhead to steady himself as he lighted it.

"All right. Relax a few minutes, finish your pipe and then go topside and give O'Mally a hand at the helm. Until the storm dies, I want two men at the tiller at all times. I'll take the second shift with Apiki, if he's able."

Darrow finished drying himself and took a cigarette from a pack on his bunk. He lighted it after some difficulty and walked to the hatch. "I'm going to see how the others are doing, then I want to inspect the ship." He looked at the cabin clock. "I'll relieve you in two hours."

Elizabeth looked up only briefly when he stepped in. She had settled Apiki in her bunk and was applying cold compresses to the wound at the side of his head.

He had bled quite freely and the pillow beneath him was spotted with the thick redness. A waste can was filled with a soiled bandage.

"How is he doing? Looks like he lost a lot of blood." Darrow shut the hatch behind him.

"I think he'll be all right. He was conscious for an hour or so. He's just sleeping now." She finished with the compresses and dabbed at the wound with a peroxide covered swab. She smeared the wound with iodine and then bandaged it with swift, confident moves. "Is everything else all right?"

"So far, so good. This typhoon is a dilly, but it most likely saved our necks. We have a little damage to the hull, but I think it's under control. I'm going to check it now." He took a puff on the cigarette and glanced around the compartment. "I thought Vargas might be here. He wasn't hurt, was he?"

She laughed, "No, he wasn't hurt, but if you want to see someone with a good case of seasickness, step into his cabin. He's the most brilliant shade of green I've ever seen."

Darrow grinned. That would keep him out of their hair for a while, anyway. He lighted a cigarette for Elizabeth and handed it to her. "You look like you could use this."

"Thanks, I've been dying for one. I lost mine somewhere. On deck, I guess." She accepted the cigarette and dragged on it eagerly, then sighed with pleasure as she exhaled. "Do you think we will be able to lose Hayama in the storm?"

"Maybe, maybe not. He has radar. If the storm doesn't jimmy it up, he should be able to track us without too much trouble. I'm not counting on it."

"Apiki was telling me that he thought we were goners for a few minutes. What if Hayama catches up with us again? Maybe we should give him what he wants. No amount of money is worth this." She looked at Apiki. "If I had thought for one minute that there were going to be people hurt, I would have destroyed that damn log page." She lowered her eyes to the deck. "It's not worth it. No amount of money." Her lips were set in bitterness,

"If I thought it would do any good, he could have the gold for all I care," Darrow said. "I agree with you completely, but you don't think that since it has gone this far, he could leave any witnesses around to testify to piracy. Not on your life. If one of us took the stand against him, even his pay off to the officials couldn't keep him from hanging." Darrow butted the cigarette in a nearby ashtray. "No, it's all or nothing for us now. Sink or swim."

He turned and slid open the door. "I'm going to check the ship. I'll be back in two hours. If Apiki is up to it by then, I'll want him to stand watch with me."

He closed the door behind him just as an exceptionally high wave rocked the ship. He lost his balance and slammed hard into the bulkhead across the corridor. Swearing and clutching his aching shoulder, he staggered to the hatch at the rear of the passageway and stepped down into the after hold.

There was still about six inches of water sloshing around inside. Bits of splinters and trash danced crazily about on its surface. The hull on the starboard side had three rough patches on it where the fifty-caliber slugs had ripped through. Adams had made hasty repairs, but when the *Malacca Maid* dipped low into the sea, the water would spurt through a gallon or so at a time.

He waded across the hold and stepped into the engine room. The door between that room and the hold was partitioned up twelve inches from the deck and the engine room had remained fairly dry. He checked quickly for damage and finding none, stepped back into the hold, closing and locking the watertight door behind him.

In the hold, heavy boxes of supplies were lashed down with one inch line. He checked these, carefully, one at a time. They were all secure until he came to the last one on the port side. A slug must have ripped through it in the battle, not severing it entirely, thank goodness, but cutting it to the point where it hung by little more than a thread. This would have to be repaired.

He climbed out of the hold and proceeded forward along the passageway in search of more line. He had almost reached the stairs leading to the deck when another heavy wave battered the ship. He grabbed at the handrail to steady himself, then stopped in mid-stride as a heavy, solid jolt shook the *Malacca Maid*. A jolt that emanated from something more than the pounding of the sea. He knew what had happened immediately.

Another heavy jolt and the *Malacca Maid* quivered beneath his feet like a dying animal in its final throes of death. The very movement sent a shiver up and down his spine. They were in for it now.

He spun sharply and bounded back down the corridor, the motion of the sea bouncing him from wall to wall as he ran. He took the steps three at a time into the after hold and the final leap dropped him into two feet of water. It was what he had feared, only worse.

The line securing the cargo on the port side had parted the rest of the way, unleashing the three tons or better of supplies that now banged dangerously, deadly, from side to side with the swaying of the ship.

CHAPTER THIRTEEN

The first damaging movements had gashed a six-inch hole in the port side and the ocean was rushing in in torrents. By the time Darrow could get to the damage, the water was almost waist high. Boxes were all over the hold, rushing from wall to wall. A crate smashed hard into his back and he went down, the salt water rushing into his throat and lungs. He came up, thrashing water, only to be swept across the hold, crashing into the starboard hull with a force that left him gasping for air.

He was on his feet again, dodging the flying crates, working his way to the damage point. He went down twice more before he was half way there. It was a useless battle.

Bart Adams tumbled down the steps and flayed his way to Darrow's side. "It's no use, Skipper. We'll never block it in time. Let's get out of here before it's too late." Adams half fell, half swam to the engine room door. He checked to see that it was secured, then started back in the direction of Darrow.

Darrow was back to the steps. As he watched, Adams was hit squarely by one of the crates. He gasped and went under, leaving only his cap floating with the debris. He surfaced again amid a turmoil of boxes and again, began working his way forward. Before he had moved five feet, Adams was down again.

Darrow extended a hand frantically, gripping the steps with the other. He groped blindly, made contact with an arm and pulled hard. Bart Adams surfaced beside him, spitting water, shaking his head in a daze.

Darrow was forced to yell to be heard over the noise. "It's no good, Bart. We'll have to get out." He pushed Adams up the steps ahead of him, then scrambled up himself. He reached the top and collapsed beside Adams.

They lay there, getting their strength, looking at each other helplessly as the hold continued to fill with water.

Adams struggled to a sitting position and leaned back against the bulkhead. "We're going to have to let her fill up and just hope she stays afloat. I don't know what else to do." He coughed the water out of his throat and spit on the deck.

"That's all we can do, Bart. The pumps won't carry the water, that's for sure. Secure this hatch and I'll have everybody stand by at the forward end of the passageway. If she starts to break up, we'll have to get off in one hell of a hurry."

Darrow staggered to his feet and swayed down the corridor to Vargas' cabin.

Vargas was in his shorts, his heavy body stretched out on the bunk. There was a puddle of vomit beside the bunk and Darrow looked at it disgustedly. Damn fool had no business on this cruise, anyway. He looked at the starry eyes and the white face and he had no pity for the man.

"Come on, buddy, on your feet. You'll make it if you're lucky." He tugged at Vargas until he had the man in a sitting position, then he buckled the life preserver around the helpless form. When Darrow released him, Vargas sank back limply against the bulkhead, then slipped off the bunk and lay prone on the floor. He rolled to one side and his mouth opened in a feeble groan.

Darrow walked to the head and filled a copper pitcher of cold water. He poured the full amount in the man's face and Vargas sputtered weakly, but didn't come around. He would have to be carried.

Darrow tried to lift him, but the swaying of the *Malacca Maid*, combined with the weakening struggle of a few moments ago in the hold, made it impossible. He finally gripped the man's wrist and dragged him across the deck out into the passageway. He dropped him by the steps and went aft to Elizabeth's cabin.

She was helping Apiki slip into a life jacket when Darrow entered. "You had better get into one of those, yourself," he urged. "Do you know what happened?" He threw a life jacket to her then helped Apiki to his feet.

"Yes, Mr. Adams just told us." Her face was white. "Is it serious?"

"Serious enough. If we're still afloat by the time this

storm blows over, I'll be surprised. I want all of you to stand by in the corridor. Don't leave your station for a second."

He helped them to their positions, then buckled on his own life jacket and staggered up the steps to the top deck.

When he opened the hatch, the wind and driving water almost knocked him from his feet. He bowed his shoulders and stepped out, protecting his eyes and face with his arms. The *Maid* was riding low in the water as he expected. Every wave now, no matter how small, was breaking over the bow and sweeping down the length of the deck. The ship was sluggish to the point that there was hardly any reaction to the tiller or the drive of the engines. If it got any worse, they would be at the mercy of the storm.

It took two men to control the tiller at this point. Adams was at one side, O'Mally on the other. Darrow tapped O'Mally on the shoulder to get his attention and yelled in his ear. "I'll take over here. You go below. If we have to abandon ship, those people in the passageway are going to need help in getting topside." He took the wheel and O'Mally went below. There was nothing to do but wait. Wait and pray.

For the first time that day, Darrow had time to think of Elizabeth. He thought of the pearly teeth, the flowing hair, black as a moonless Oriental night. He thought of the flashing black eyes, the determined set of the mouth and jaw. He could see the snowy mounts that were her breasts, rising and falling with her passionate breath. He could feel the silken smoothness of her slim thighs beneath his hands.

He cursed himself mentally, angry at his own desires. It was desire, he knew that. Love hadn't entered the picture as yet. Maybe it never would. There was a fondness, of course. A strong bond of friendship, that was all. But he wanted her. He wanted this girl like he had never wanted anything in his life.

He was brought back to reality by a sudden slackening in their forward motion. The engines had stopped. He knew what had happened immediately. The engine room was flooding. Water had reached the engines and drowned them out. Adams looked at him fearfully and Darrow knew that he, too, realized what had happened.

This was the end of the *Malacca Maid*. With the engines dead and no forward motion, it was impossible to steer. They would have to leave the ship.

The *Malacca Maid* fell into a trough, turned broadside to the storm and took the next wave full against her port side. Darrow's heart sank as the main lifeboat was torn from its boom and went sweeping across the deck, taking everything in its path with it to a watery grave.

The next wave splintered the mizzenmast and the one after that ripped away the temporary lines they had used to tie it down. In the next instant, it was sent crashing to the deck, ending up in a twisted mass of lines and rubble, its tip extending twenty feet out over the starboard rail.

Darrow gripped Adams' shoulder and yelled in his ear. "We might as well kiss the old girl goodbye. She can't take much more of this."

Adams nodded gravely and looked away. She was a

good ship, but she was dying. It was like seeing an old friend die.

The two men waited, crouched behind the helm, until the next wave crashed over them, then dashed for the hatch. The others were standing at the foot of the steps, their necks craned, their eyes watching the hatch anxiously.

Darrow stepped down after Adams, closing the hatch behind him so that he could be heard. "We're going to have to abandon ship. The main lifeboat has been swept away and the sea is too rough to lower the small one. We'll have to depend on the life jackets." He uncoiled a length of line from the deck of the passageway and handed it down the line. "Each of you fasten this around your waists. Our only chance, once we hit the water, is to stay together. Bart, use the emergency set and send out our position. We'll wait for you here. We still have a few minutes."

Adams disappeared into a doorway and Darrow looked at the others. There was no fear in their faces. At least no more than there must have been in his own. It was a good crew and they were good passengers. Even Vargas had recovered from his seasickness and seemed to be bearing up as well as could be expected.

Darrow hooked an arm around Elizabeth's waist and pulled her to his side, reassuringly. She looked up at him and smiled, but there were tears in her eyes. "When they hear our distress signal, John, how long will it take to reach us?"

Darrow stared at the deck. He might as well level with them.

When he spoke, he raised his voice so that all could hear. "This ship carries a wireless with a five-hundred-mile range. Unfortunately, when the engines flooded, it became useless because of lack of power. The lights below deck are running on an emergency power pack. One too small to run the main radio on. We are going to have to use the smaller emergency set. It has a range of a hundred miles at best. We can only hope that there is a ship in the area. A ship other than Hayama's, that is." He said nothing, after that. There was nothing to say.

Adams came back from the radio room. "I sent the SOS for three minutes, Skipper. If they didn't hear it in that time, they're not likely to at all."

Darrow nodded and led the way up the steps. He slid open the hatch and stepped out onto deck, the others filing after him. For a full minute, no one spoke. They stared around them in awe.

Bart Adams broke the silence. "Good, God! Good, God All Mighty! The storm's gone!"

CHAPTER FOURTEEN

Apiki began to sob softly, fingering the rosary at his neck. The wind had died to a soft breeze, the rain has stopped, the waters around them were once more smooth as glass. Overhead the sky was a brilliant blue. It was like being reborn. Fresh life being forced into their lungs.

Darrow surveyed the situation grimly, then turned to face them. The gods were cruel sometime. "It's only a postponement of the end, I'm afraid. We're not out of the storm, we're in the eye. There's more to come. The only real break is that we can lower the small boat now."

"Damn good thing, too." It was O'Mally who spoke and as he did so, he waved an arm at the seas around them. Deadly black fins circled the boat, darting back and forth rapidly in the water. Sharks! They wouldn't last two minutes without a boat.

Adams pressed forward, stripping the rope from around his waist. "Skipper, there is one thing we can do. At least try!" He hesitated as everyone gathered around eagerly. "God knows how long we'll be in the eye. Maybe twenty minutes, maybe an hour. If we can get that gash in the hold repaired, we may have time to pump it out. After that we can dry off the engines and maybe weather this damn storm."

"It's no good, Bart," Darrow cut in. "We'd have to go in the water to get at the hole and a swimmer wouldn't last a minute with those sharks around."

"From the inside, Skipper. From the inside. We have SCUBA gear aboard. A man could drop into the hold with lungs on his back, find the hole and slap a temporary patch on it in twenty minutes. I'd like permission to at least take a crack at the job. If I'm not done by the time the storm moves back in on us, signal me and I'll come up. We would still have time to lower the lifeboat." Adams chewed nervously on the unlit pipe.

Darrow slapped his leg excitedly. "By God, Bart, you've hit on it. The chances are slim, but there is a chance. I'm going to do the diving myself, though. It's my ship and if anyone is going to risk their neck for it, it's going to be me. Haul out the SCUBA gear." Darrow began to shed his clothes quickly.

Adams bounded below and came up shortly with the breathing apparatus and the underwater lantern.

Darrow strapped it on hurriedly, barking instructions. "O'Mally, chop away that mess around the mast and drop it overboard, mast and all. The way it is now, it throws us out of balance. Apiki, stand by the pumps and as soon as I signal, start them up. Bart, you come with me in case I run into trouble. Vargas, give O'Mally a hand with the mast. Elizabeth, you can start loading supplies from the galley into the lifeboat, just in case. Come on, Bart. If this works, I'll buy you the biggest steak you ever had when we get back to port!" The two men stepped down into the passageway and moved back to the after hold. They opened the hatch cautiously and the black water bubbled over the rim of the hatch and onto the deck of the corridor. Darrow adjusted the breathing tube and dropped into the hole. Adams closed and locked the hatch when he had disappeared, holding back the rising sea.

Inside, there was utter darkness. Darrow flicked the switch on the lantern and flashed the dim ray around the interior, orienting himself. The lighter crates had floated against the top of the hold, the others lay strewn about the watery deck. He clutched the patching equipment to his side and glided the short distance through the debris to the gash in the port side. Small fish darted excitedly back and forth as he swam through them. Darrow set the lantern on a large crate and went to work immediately on the hole. He knocked away the jagged edges quickly and slipped the eighteen-inch square aluminum patch into place. He began to drill feverishly, never stopping until the last hole was ready for the screws. It was another ten minutes before the job was done.

He returned to the hatch and rapped on the underside three times, the signal to start the pumps.

There was still work to be done. The two patches that Bart had made over the bullet holes would have to be repaired.

The pumps cut in shortly with a deep rumble that resounded through the water filled hold. Darrow worked steadily on the patches while the water level began to slowly recede. By the time they were fixed to his satisfaction, the water had dropped to shoulder level and the floating crates began to settle slowly to the deck. It looked as though they might make it.

Twenty minutes more and there was only two feet of water left. Adams dropped down from the corridor and they began to restack and secure the jumbled crates. Those that had broken, they emptied of their contents and dropped over the side, storing those supplies that could be salvaged in the galley.

O'Mally and Apiki came below and, under the supervision of Adams, set about drying the engines off as rapidly as possible.

Darrow returned topside and watched the approaching wall of the storm with an experienced eye. Their luck had been good. The eye of the storm had remained around them for an hour, but now the skies were darkening and the wind had started to whip the white caps to life. They would have five, maybe ten minutes at the most.

As he waited, Darrow looked around sadly at his once proud ship. She had taken an almost fatal beating and it showed. The mizzenmast had been dropped overboard, Vargas was cutting away the loose lines and dumping them. The starboard rail had been swept away by the main lifeboat and the hatches and deck were splintered here and there where they had been raked by the fifty-caliber. The Malacca Maid was still afloat, but that was all you could say.

The engines coughed and sputtered uncertainly and then roared to life as the rising wind drove the first drops of rain across the water and splattered them against the *Malacca Maid*.

Adams returned from below decks and he and Darrow manned the tiller. Another three minutes and the second half of the typhoon was on them with all its fury.

CHAPTER FIFTEEN

The storm passed over them at four o'clock the next morning, leaving behind a battered ship and an exhausted crew.

Vargas had become seasick a second time and now lay weakly below deck, his body drained of strength and fluids.

Elizabeth McClain had cared for the wounded Apiki until almost midnight and then had dragged herself wearily to an empty bunk where she now slept.

John Darrow had slept for not quite four hours after the peak of the storm had passed and, fifteen minutes before, had relieved Adams and O'Mally at the helm.

He was alone on deck. The exhaustion brought about by the events of the last three days or so still plagued his body. His eyes were red rimmed and sunken, circled with dark shadows of fatigue. The others were in the same condition as he was. There would have to be a let up soon, or the strain might prove disastrous.

Now, however, there was another problem that had presented itself. A mental problem, rather than physical, this time. It was the *Malacca Maid*. At this point, she could hardly be called seaworthy. True, she was afloat and she would stay afloat, providing they hit no more storms. Had it been a different time of year, Darrow would have gone on to the site of the *Mary Owen* without hesitation. But, this was the typhoon season. The next one might blow up today, tomorrow, next week or next month, there was no telling. The only thing that was for certain, was that the *Malacca Maid* would never ride out another one in her condition. They would have to stop for repairs.

Putting in to shore, on the other hand, would mean a delay of at least a week. Of course, the delay was only secondary. The main danger lay in what was behind them. Suto Hayama! The possibility that his junk had been sunk in the storm was too much to hope for. Not knowing one way or the other, they would have to figure him in any plans they made.

Darrow tried to put himself in Hayama's shoes. They had lost the *Malacca Maid* in the typhoon. It would be an impossibility to sweep the seas, hoping to pick up their trail by chance. The only thing left, the one last chance, would be to search the harbors along Luzon and Mindoro in the faint hope that the *Malacca Maid* had been damaged and was forced to put ashore.

It was true that there were many harbors, but there were only three, maybe four, where it would be possible to obtain the material necessary to make anything but the most minor repairs.

It was a simple deduction, Darrow decided. If they put in to shore, Hayama would be on their backs in no time at all. Yet, there was no choice. If they didn't put in and another typhoon blew up, they might as well start blowing up their water wings, because they were sure to get their feet wet. Of course, if Hayama did find them, he could do nothing in a Philippine port. What he would undoubtedly do, would be to sit at anchor outside the harbor and wait for them to put to sea. Then, they would pick up where they had left off before the last storm. Darrow didn't relish the idea in the least bit.

Darrow locked the tiller in position and pulled the sextant from its place by the helm. The sun would be up in a few minutes and he wanted to get a fix from the stars before dawn broke. A few checks, sightings, double checks, a little quick figuring, and he had their position. They had been blown almost seventy-five miles off course. As near as he could figure, they were about fifty to fifty-five miles northeast of Limit Point on Luzon, and about thirty-five miles north of Lubang Island.

Paluan, on the northern tip of Mindoro, would be their best bet. It wasn't far off their course and there was a fair-sized boatyard there. Darrow unlocked the tiller and headed the bow into the southwest. They would circle west of Lubang Island and hit Mindoro by noon of that day.

No one stirred below decks until almost ten o'clock that morning. The sun was high and hot in the unbroken blueness of the Philippine sky and, with the help of a slight southerly current, the *Malacca Maid* had made good time.

Bart Adams poked his sunburned head out of the hatch first. He blinked his eyes and squinted into the sudden brightness, then stepped all the way on deck and joined Darrow at the tiller. "I'll take over now, Skipper. That six-hour sleep was the most I've had at one time for a week. I feel like a million bucks."

"Maybe I should have routed you out. I'll be damned if I want a spoiled First Mate on my hands," Darrow grinned and stepped back from the helm.

Adams checked the course, locked the wheel and pulled out the battered pipe, filling it methodically. The *Malacca Maid* was passing through the channel that separated Luzon on the east and Lubang on the west. The land mass of each could be seen on the horizons to port and to starboard.

Adams finished filling the pipe and then struck a match to it, shielding the fire from the wind with a calloused and somewhat dirty hand. "I'd say, offhand, we're headin' for Paluan. That right, Skipper?"

"It was the best place I could think of to put in. It'll be about two hours yet."

"Good a place as any, I guess. You haven't seen her for some time now. What was her name again? Daisy?

Denise? A real doll, as I recall," Adams chuckled.

"Seems to me like it's a little risky, though," Adams laughed loudly now.

"Last time we left Paluan, you come down the dock like a bear out of a bee tree. I heard you yellin' for me to get underway while you were still two blocks away!" Adams was trying to muffle his laughter and his whole body was shaking convulsively. "We pulled away from the pier, you made a long dive and landed flat on your face on deck. This gal's father and her three brothers was a little late and instead of landing on the *Maid*, they all missed the deck and landed in the drink. You never did tell me what happened, but since you were only wearing your shorts and a tee shirt, I had a pretty good idea." Darrow grinned and faked a punch at his First Mate. "You foul-minded old bastard. They just came down to wish me Bon Voyage." His face flushed and the grin widened as he recalled the full details of the episode. "I'm not calling on her this trip. As a matter of fact, I'm not even going into town. We're going to drop anchor in that inlet across the peninsula and you'll have to take the boys into town for whatever we need. If I pulled the *Malacca Maid* into Paluan Bay, Hayama would spot us for sure."

Adams sputtered and yanked the pipe from his mouth.

"You mean we got to haul a new mast clear across the damned island?" He replaced the pipe and clamped his teeth down on it angrily, frowning at Darrow.

"It's not as bad as all that. If you look hard enough, you can borrow a truck someplace. I figure, with a week of good, hard work, we'll have her back in shipshape and we can get under way again."

Adams nodded his agreement, still frowning. "I guess you're right. We've lost the piratical bastard for a while. No use asking for trouble."

A little after noon, the *Malacca Maid* pulled into an unnamed cove a few miles to the west of Del Monte Point. It was the perfect place to remain undetected. A narrow and shallow channel ran a hundred feet or so from the ocean, then billowed out into somewhat the shape of a horse's head, perhaps five hundred yards long and from a hundred and fifty to three hundred yards in width. A shallow beach circled the cove and in from the beach, the jungle was thick and green. The channel entrance curved so that a ship, at anchor in the cove, was completely hidden from the sea. Due to the limited depth of the water, it was not possible to anchor closer than a hundred yards from shore.

The *Malacca Maid* entered the cove slowly, Darrow at the helm, and Adams at the bow, taking soundings in the shallow channel. Several times the sound of the sharp coral scrapings against the hull grated in their ears, but there was little or no damage. For the time being at least, they could relax.

When they dropped anchor, no one spoke at first. The utter silence of the moment was broken only by the gentle lapping of the water against the hull and the excited screeching of the birds and monkeys in the nearby jungle. They had been close to death more times than they cared to remember in the past days and, possibly, they would come even closer in the future. But now there was serenity, tranquility, an overpowering sense of joy, a love of life that overcame all else. The thought of the twelve million dollars locked in the hold of the *Mary Owen* suddenly became unimportant.

Darrow broke the silence, raising his voice so that all could hear. "We'll rest for the remainder of the day. It's too late to get started anyway. Crap out, swim, do as you like." He nodded at Adams. "Break out a couple bottles of scotch. I think we could all do with a drink. Tomorrow, we'll start patching the old girl up."

The group scattered, all but Elizabeth following Adams to the liquor cabinet.

Darrow leaned lazily against the rail, his eyes surveying the ship slowly, his mind noting methodically the repairs that would have to be made and the supplies that would be needed. If she ever looked the same again, it would be a miracle.

Elizabeth joined him, pulling a crumpled pack of cigarettes from the pocket of her white blouse. She took one, gave one to Darrow and said, "She took quite a beating, didn't she. I didn't think it would be possible to survive that. I guess a ship is like a human body. You never know how much it can take, until something like this happens. Then you can't bring yourself to believe it."

"Speaking of bodies, mine's dirty." He lighted his cigarette, then hers. "I'm going to take a quick dip and then I'm going to sleep until tomorrow morning and if anybody dares to wake me for anything less than World War III, there'll be hell to pay. Want to join me? Swimming, I mean!"

"If we were alone, John, I'd join you in bed, too. Since

we're not, though, a swim would be nice." Her eyes teased him, signaled a promise of what could not be. At least not this time.

CHAPTER SIXTEEN

The water was cool, refreshing. Darrow dove deep and she followed, down twenty, then thirty feet, gliding easily in and out among the pink coral and the swaying vegetation that reached skyward from the floor of the cove. The fishes darted back and forth curiously about them, their unblinking eyes staring in wonderment at the strange creatures that dared invade their domain. The two creatures that locked themselves in each other's arms, pressed their lips together, then parted and shot upward to the surface, laughter bubbling from their mouths as they broke water.

They swam lazily for ten, perhaps fifteen minutes, slowly working their way closer to the beach. Finally, they stretched out, belly down, on the white sand. Darrow glanced quickly back at the *Malacca Maid*, and the deck was deserted. He reached over and gathered her in his arms, pressing his mouth to hers hungrily.

Elizabeth responded warmly, her breath growing short and rapid. Then she pushed him away and laid back. "Please," she gasped. "I have to admit I like it, but someone might see us. Tch, tch. Disgraceful conduct." She giggled and, grasping his hand, pulled it to her face. "Aren't you ever too tired for love?"

He grinned and with his free hand, brushed some of the white sand off of his leg. "I've been too tired to eat, too tired to sleep and too tired to drink, but I've never been too tired to fight or make love."

He looked again at the *Malacca Maid* and this time, Vargas had come on deck. He was leaning on the port rail watching the shore line.

Darrow rolled to his back, shielded his eyes from the sun with his forearm and dropped off almost immediately to sleep. It had been a long day.

When he awoke, she was gone and so was the sun. Darrow checked his watch and to his surprise, found that it was three thirty in the morning. He was in the same position as he had gone to sleep fourteen hours previously.

He yawned and staggered stiffly to his feet, the stiffness in his joints causing him to reflect that he wasn't as young as he used to be.

The beach was cold in the absence of the sun and he shivered, swinging his arms to speed the circulation. He looked out across the cove and he could barely make out the outline of the *Malacca Maid* against the dim light of the sky. "Well," he thought, "there's work to be done," and he stepped into the water. He swam slowly, easily, taking advantage of the time to clear his head. He might as well rout the others out right away he thought. The sooner they started, the better. The initial enchantment of the secluded cove had worn off and he found himself thinking eagerly once again of the *Mary Owen*.

Once aboard the *Malacca Maid*, he woke the others, then went to his cabin and showered and shaved.

When he had finished, he dressed in a fresh pair of white ducks and made his way to the galley. For the first time, he felt refreshed, ready for anything. The sleep had been just what the doctor ordered.

Elizabeth was alone in the galley, putting the final touches on a fresh pot of coffee. She smiled when he came in. "You looked so peaceful there on the beach, I didn't want to disturb you so I came back alone. I hope you slept well."

"Slept like a log and I feel like a million bucks. All I need now is a cigarette, a cup of that coffee and two or three eggs." He swung a chair around, settled down on it backward and rested his chin on its back, while Elizabeth poured the coffee.

Adams came in then, followed by Apiki and O'Mally. Vargas entered five minutes later. A quick breakfast, a little sleepy conversation, and the day had begun.

There was a trail, an ox road actually, leading across the peninsula to Paluan and by the time the sun came up, the crew of the *Malacca Maid* and a grumbling Vargas were well on their way.

Darrow set about removing the rigging from the remaining mast as soon as it was light enough to see. Most of it was too far gone to salvage and that he dumped overboard.

Darrow was thinking of Vargas while he worked. Perhaps he had been too rough on the man. Since the time he came aboard, Darrow had given him every dirty job that came along. He had done them and done them well. He had grumbled but, Darrow reflected, so would anyone. He hadn't really given the man a chance.

Darrow lighted a cigarette and stepped back from his work. He owed Vargas an apology. It was about time he stopped acting like a spoiled child and gave the man a break. They would be back from Paluan in the early evening and Darrow would have to talk to the man. Humbleness had never been one of Darrow's strong points, but every now and then it became necessary. This was one of those times.

By noon, he had cleared the tangled wreckage from the deck and was working on the bolts and braces that secured the splintered stump of the mizzenmast. The midday sun was draining the moisture from his body and after only a few short minutes, he had stripped to his shorts.

At one o'clock, Elizabeth came topside with a refreshing mixture of gin and tonic. "Take a break, John. The *Mary Owen* isn't going anyplace. I thought maybe you would appreciate one of these."

She handed him the frosted glass and he relaxed against the forward hatch, swishing the first sip around gingerly in his parched mouth. He swallowed and sighed contentedly. "It hits the spot all right." He swallowed again and the drink was half gone. "I've been thinking. How about a swim before lunch?"

"Fine with me. I'm not too hungry yet. I suppose you're starved, though."

"Not too bad. I'll tell you what, you pack a lunch and mix a pitcher of gin and tonic. We can take the dingy to shore and I know where there's a fresh water pool just through the jungle a quarter of a mile or so. While you're doing that, I'll finish ripping out what's left of the mizzenmast." He took a final swallow of the drink and returned the empty glass to Elizabeth.

She disappeared through the hatch and Darrow returned to work on the mizzenmast. It would be a half hour or so before she would be ready.

They pulled the dingy well up on the shore and Darrow searched only briefly before he found the shaded trail that wound its way back into the jungle. It was an old native trail, seldom used and almost grown over by the spreading vines and roots that seemed to spring up overnight from the moist, black floor of the jungle.

In the trees above them, a corps of monkeys darted excitedly from limb to limb, keeping just ahead of them and stopping from time to time to ogle the strange intruders. They would perch on the high branches and twist their necks to stare over their backs, their eyes wide and curious, their tails twitching nervously.

They walked for perhaps ten minutes before they could hear the roar of cascading water and another five minutes before they came upon the pool itself.

A waterfall tumbled sixty feet down a rocky bluff and reached a thundering end fifty feet from where they stood, filling the air with a fine spray that drenched the surrounding shrubbery. The pool was possibly fifty by a hundred feet, dropping off at the downstream end to another set of falls that continued on to the sea. Multi-colored orchids and sampaguita grew in abundance on all sides and filled the air with a breathtaking fragrance.

"Oh, John, it's beautiful. I've never seen anything so lovely," she said.

"It is great, isn't it. I came upon it quite by accident one day about six years ago. This is the only time I've ever been back. I always meant to, but somehow I never quite made it."

He set the lunch basket on the mossy bank and squatted beside it, undoing the buttons on his shirt.

Elizabeth dipped one of her bare feet into the water's edge and withdrew it quickly. The water was cold. Much colder than the lagoon.

Her blouse came off in one swift motion and a second later her shorts were crumpled around her feet. She stood that way for a moment, letting Darrow stare longingly at the gentle curves of her body, then she climbed quickly to a nearby rock. Her body arched gracefully and she hit the water with hardly a ripple.

Darrow followed almost immediately. He dived to twelve, maybe fifteen feet before he found her, gliding gracefully along the sandy bottom. They joined hands and surfaced in the center of the pool, the lily pads parting easily to let them rise.

Darrow gathered her roughly in his arms and kissed her, long and hard. She rolled to her back and let him tow her back to shore.

Overhead the monkeys chattered excitedly, but Darrow never heard them.

CHAPTER SEVENTEEN

It was a full ten days before the *Malacca Maid* was ready to sail again. She was still ragged in spots, her paint job was rough, the main lifeboat still had not been replaced and the bullet holes in her cabin and deck still remained as a grim reminder of what had happened. Most important of all, her holds were dry and the once flooded engines were again purring like a pair of contented kittens.

No one had returned to Paluan since the first day, but now it would be necessary to return the borrowed truck and Darrow felt that the crew had earned a night on the town. It could also be true that he wanted another chance to be alone with Elizabeth. As it turned out, Vargas remained aboard the *Maid* also, and whatever plans Darrow may have had failed to materialize.

The best laid plans of mice and men oft go astray. Darrow was sleeping when they came back and he awoke to find Adams shaking him roughly. "Skipper. Skipper, wake up. We've got trouble."

Darrow rolled over and grumbled sleepily. He rubbed at his eyes to clear them and checked his watch. It was two thirty. "What the hell?" He sat up quickly and swung his feet to the deck. "What happened, Bart?"

"Well, we did like you said. Everyone stayed together and we hit this one bar on the outskirts of town and stayed there all night." Adams fumbled for a match, found one and struck it to his pipe. "We were sitting in a booth in a dark corner sippin' a few and watching the floor show, when four of Hayama's men came in. They just pushed through the door and looked the place over, then turned around and left. As soon as they had gone, we beat it out the back door and set a course for the *Malacca Maid*. I'm not sure they saw us, it was pretty dark in there. The thing is they could have. I thought you'd want to know right away." He started to pace the floor nervously.

Darrow swore softly at the turn of bad luck. He fumbled in the darkened cabin for his cigarettes. "How long ago was this?"

"Must have been about eleven o'clock, maybe eleven thirty. We came back as fast as we could. Apiki hung back a bit to make sure no one followed us."

Darrow found the cigarettes and lighted one. His face was troubled in the flickering light of the match. He remained silent for a while, puffing deeply on the cigarette and turning everything over in his mind. There was only one thing to do. They would have to get under way immediately.

"All right, Bart. We'd better pull the hook and get our tail out of here. Let the crew sack out, you and I can handle it alone. Get the engines started and I'll get to the helm as soon as I dress."

Adams left and Darrow began lacing his shoes hurriedly. It would be a tricky bit of navigation to get through the channel in the dark, but they would have to make a try at it. Adams was certain that no one had followed them when they returned to the ship, but if by chance they had been, and the *Malacca Maid* sat it out until daylight, Hayama could bottle them up in the lagoon and there would be hell to pay. No, they would have to try tonight.

Darrow buttoned on his shirt and pants quickly and went out on deck. It was going to be a more tricky job than he thought. A heavy fog had settled, blanket-like, over the water and visibility had been cut to no more than fifty feet.

The engines came to life with a deep rumble that set the deck to vibrating beneath his feet. Darrow searched in the cabin and came up with the sounding line. When he returned to the helm, Adams had come up from the engine room.

"Skipper, if you get the old girl out of here in this pea soup, I'll eat my new pair of dress shoes. Don't you think we should wait 'til morning?" His voice was a hollow echo in the dense fog and the bowl of the pipe glowed dimly in the night.

"No dice, Bart. I want to be heading into the Mindoro Strait by dawn." He handed his first mate the sounding line. "I'll cut the screws down as slow as I can and you give me a sounding every ten seconds. I'm hoping that if we do run up on the rocks, our speed will be too slow to do any damage." He took a final puff on the cigarette and flipped it over the side.

Adams turned toward the bow and by the time he reached it, his figure was almost obliterated by the fog and darkness. He waved his arm in a signal for Darrow to get under way.

Darrow started the winch and the anchor chain clinked and rattled noisily as it was pulled aboard. He engaged the clutch and the *Malacca Maid* churned slowly into the fog. Darrow spun the wheel and they made a ninety degree turn in the direction of the channel.

The trees loomed darkly on each side of them as they entered the narrow passageway and Darrow heard the faint splash as the sounding line was dropped over the bow. "Four fathoms," the call echoed back through the fog. "Three fathoms. Hold it, back off. A little bit to port. O.K., you're all right. Keep her coming...."

"Two fathoms."

"Five feet. Easy now."

Coral scraped sharply along the port side and Darrow pulled the bow to starboard. Somewhere, off in the night, a gull screeched loudly. Ahead of them, the surf roared angrily as it crashed upon the rocky beach. The sounding line dropped over the bow again and hit the water with a soft splash. Adams' reports rang back at ten second intervals from the direction of the bow.

In twenty minutes, they had cleared the channel and Darrow pushed the engines to ahead two-thirds. The ocean slapped sharply against the hull and the *Malacca Maid* began to rise and fall in the shallow ground swells.

Adams came aft and stationed himself beside Darrow at the helm. "Well, Skipper. Those shoes of mine are going to go down awful hard. If you forget what I said about eatin' them, I might consider buying you a drink when we get back to Macao. On second thought, I'll buy you a dozen of 'em!"

"It's a deal," he laughed. "You already owe me a steak. I'll have to have the boys keep an eye on you to see that you don't jump ship before I take you up on it." Darrow stepped aside and looked at his watch. It was three fifteen. "Take the wheel and keep her on this course until four thirty. Then put her nose dead on two seventy degrees. I'm going back to the sack."

He left Adams and stepped through the hatch, the

bulb in the passageway having burned out, and he felt along the wall gingerly until he found the door to his cabin. He cursed himself under his breath. He would have to remember to get that replaced.

Once inside, he stretched out on the bunk without bothering to undress. He realized that his body was as tense as spring steel from the trip through the channel and he made a conscious effort to relax.

He folded the pillow under his head and closed his eyes. No good. He turned over on one side and doubled his knees up against him. Still no good. He was wide-awake, like it or not. Elizabeth's face and lovely body flashed through his mind and he knew then that he was through sleeping for certain.

He rolled out of the bunk and walked to the head. Cold water gurgled into the wash basin and he splashed his face and hair vigorously. He ran his fingers over the stubble on his chin and decided against shaving. He had a two-day growth now, one more day wouldn't matter. He brushed his teeth and gargled with an antiseptic smelling liquid. Might as well start the day.

When he was through washing, he made his way to the galley and started the morning pot of coffee. He decided to hell with the slow, drip method and once the water was boiling, he dumped the grounds directly into it. To Darrow, it was much better this way. You might walk around all morning spitting coffee grounds from between your teeth, but while you were drinking it, it was real coffee!

He took the whole pot back to his cabin and set it on the desk that folded down out of the bulkhead. They would arrive at the sight of the sinking that night around dark and this would be as good a time as any to plan the search pattern. He pulled paper and pen out of a drawer and flicked on the Trans-Oceanic radio. Might as well have music while he worked.

The only local charts that he could locate of the area had been made in 1936. Their accuracy was doubtful, but they would have to do. The charts indicated the depth in that area to vary from twenty to fifty fathoms, with the exception of one area that was marked unknown. A valley that ran from north to south along the Eastern rim of the pattern. The unknown label would indicate depths of over six hundred fathoms. If it was down there, they might as well kiss it goodbye right now.

The search, if they had to complete the pattern before finding the *Mary Owen*, would take about four to six weeks. The twenty fathom depths would be easy, taking perhaps a week to cover. There, he could use Adams and perhaps Apiki. After that, he would have to go it alone, as none of the others had the experience to venture safely beyond that depth.

In the fifty fathom depths, the days would be long and the going extremely slow. Working, as they were, without a decompression tank, the maximum amount of searching time would be forty to forty-five minutes. Maybe an hour, at the most. He would be forced to make nine decompression stops between the bottom and the surface. There was no way to get around it. No way to get around it and still live, that is. He had seen men with the bends before. There were a million ways to die that were less painful.

There was still another problem. Even with the double tanks they would be using, the air supply would last four hours at the most. Sometime during the decompression stops, he would have to change tanks. That would be at about the thirty-foot level, if he stretched it. They only carried two sets of tanks aboard the *Malacca Maid*. Therefore, the person who brought down the spare tanks would have to free dive. If, for one reason or another, he was to run out of air at the deeper level, he would be sunk. There would be no way to get the spare tank down to him. It was going to be a touch and go operation to say the least.

The Manila radio station blared out their version of "Tennessee Waltz," then cut it short and a Spanish speaking announcer came on the air with an advertisement plugging a local fertilizer that was supposed to be far superior to the age-old method of saving the human movements and throwing them on the rice fields in the spring. There was little or no smell, it was more sanitary and it was chemically treated to restore the necessary minerals to the soil.

Darrow finished his coffee and poured a fresh cup. That was one reason he had never had much of a taste for Oriental grown rice.

His stomach growled hungrily and he wished to hell Elizabeth would get up and start breakfast. He played with the idea of waking her for a moment, then dropped it. If he went in there, they would most likely both wind up in the sack and the whole morning would be shot. Not that it wouldn't be worth it, but there was too much to be done. Far too much. One of these days though, whether they found the gold or not, he was going to take off a month or so. He figured he wouldn't have too much trouble in persuading Elizabeth to take a little cruise. To the South Pacific, maybe. They'd find a quiet little island, perhaps Tahiti, rent a cottage, have the meals brought in, bar the door and windows and never get out of the sack for a month. Bart Adams had told him once that his favorite breakfast was, "a roll in bed with honey." Darrow wasn't sure if you could live on that, but he was sure as hell going to have a go at it.

The announcer finished with the advertisement and put a screechy rock 'n' roll tune on the disc. Darrow flicked off the radio disgustedly and lighted a cigarette. To hell with that crap. He suffered enough in normal, everyday living, without having to listen to that.

Way off in the distance, a fog horn blasted forth hollowly in a mournful cry of warning. Darrow glanced at his watch. They would be entering the Apo East Pass of the Mindoro Straits. He stepped to the porthole and opened it. The fog rolled into the cabin in faint, moist wisps and outside there was nothing, utter darkness. Not even a light blinking from the islands that he knew were nearby. The soup was so thick, you could cut it with a knife.

The air was cool and refreshing anyway, and he took a couple of deep breaths before returning to the desk, leaving the porthole standing open. He often wondered why a man that enjoyed fresh air as much as he did, ever smoked so many of those damn coffin nails. One of these days he was going to quit.

By six o'clock, he finished the plan for the search pattern and went on deck. The fog had lifted to a certain extent, but still hung, blanket-like, at five or six hundred feet above the water. The chill morning air seeped through his thin clothing and he shivered, wishing he had thought to don a jacket.

He picked up the binoculars and swept the horizon methodically. To the east, the dim outline of southern Mindoro poked its mountainous head through the overcast and stared back at him blackly. A small fishing boat rocked at anchor in the swells a mile or so away, but there was no sign of Hayama's junk. Darrow still had the feeling he was out there, tracking them.

"Get your sleep-out?" It was Adams that spoke, his voice thick and gravelly from the many years of sucking on the charred bowl he called a pipe.

"Who the hell slept? I just finished charting our search pattern once we reach our destination. You feel like doing a little SCUBA work once we get there?"

"What the hell do you mean, 'Do I feel like it?' Sonny, I was diving while you were still crappin' yellow." He growled something else that Darrow couldn't make out and sucked harder on the pipe. "You just give Ol' Bart the word and I'll make you young squirts look like a bunch of amateurs."

"O.K., O.K., take it easy you old buzzard," Darrow chuckled. "Don't get your dander up. I'll have you under water so much, you'll start growing fins." He walked over and checked their course. It was right on the button.

Vargas came on deck a few minutes later and he and Darrow talked shortly. Darrow had almost choked on his tongue a few days prior to that, but he had managed to bark out a gruff apology for his actions earlier in the cruise. Since that time, their relationship, while still cool, had improved considerably.

"What time do you think we'll get there?" he had asked.

"I figure about six, maybe seven o'clock," Darrow replied. "We'll start diving at dawn tomorrow, weather permitting, that is." He pulled a jacket from inside the hatch and slipped into it, zipping it half way to the top.

Vargas pulled a cigar from his coat pocket and removed the cellophane from it slowly. "Once we find the *Mary Owen*, if we find it, how long will it take to salvage the gold?" He bit off the tip of the cigar and spit it over the side.

"Hard to say. It all depends on how she's laying. With luck, we could have the gold on board the *Malacca Maid* in three hours. Without luck, it might take a week. I wouldn't start counting it yet, if I were you."

"I believe I mentioned once before, Captain, that I'm not interested in the gold for myself. I'm only here to protect Elizabeth's interests." He struck a match and held it to the cigar, drawing deeply.

"Yeah, I believe you did say something like that. I suppose if she offered you a million or so, you'd turn it down cold." Darrow lighted a cigarette.

"Like you said, Captain. Let's not start counting it yet."

"Yeah, like I said, let's not start counting it." He turned and walked off slowly, leaving Vargas standing alone at the rail. Why was it that every time the two of them talked, they parted on a disagreeable note such as this? "Oh, what the hell. The bastard won't be hanging around forever," he thought.

The heavy ceiling of fog hung over them all the rest of that day and at seven o'clock that evening, Darrow dropped the sea anchor. They were reasonably close to the desired position, but it would be impossible to pinpoint it exactly until the fog lifted and he was able to get a fix on either the sun or stars. By dark, the fog rather than lifting, had closed in even more thickly around them.

They were close now, too close to think of anything but twelve million dollars. Dinner that night was eaten with hardly a word being spoken. They stared at their plates and ate automatically, picking indifferently at the food before them. After that, they left the table one by one, each absorbed in his own thoughts, seeking to disassociate themselves from each other.

"So this is gold fever," Darrow thought. He had heard men speak of it, he had read of it, and now he was seeing it for the first time. He even had it himself to a certain extent. It was a fever that gripped men's minds. More than that, worse than that, it gripped their souls. It wasn't pleasant to see and it was worse to feel as it crept in and slowly enveloped his own brain.

Darrow shook it off with an effort and turned his mind to other matters. He had read accounts of normal human beings, swept up by the fever and turned to little more than animals. Secretive, distrustful. Ready to kill for it. Ready to die for it. He could only hope it didn't happen on the *Malacca Maid*.

He forced himself to consider Hayama. This would be the most dangerous time. From this point, until they were through diving. They would have to maintain a watch around the clock. One moment of carelessness could, and very likely would, prove fatal. He would venture to say there was gold fever aboard Hayama's vessel tonight also, wherever it was.

CHAPTER EIGHTEEN

The deck was deserted when he went topside and he decided to take the first watch himself. He would stay there until twelve o'clock, maybe get a fix on their position if the stars came out and then wake someone, probably Apiki, to relieve him. After that, he would alternate the watch every three hours.

The BAR was still below and he brought it topside and mounted it on top of the deck cabin. It had saved their necks once before and they might have to put it to use again at any hour, at any minute. He patted it fondly and covered it with a tarp before jumping down from the cabin top.

He picked up the binoculars and swept the horizon once again. There was nothing in sight as far as he could see, which wasn't very far. The water was relatively calm and the only sound was from the gentle lapping of the waves against the hull of the *Malacca Maid*.

The watch was going to be a long one and he hoped, uneventful.

At eleven o'clock the fog was as thick as ever and he

still hadn't been able to get a fix on their position. He dragged slowly on a cigarette and rested against the rail that surrounded the helm on three sides. Suddenly he was aware of a movement by the hatch entrance. He froze and melted back into the shadows of the cabin, curious as to what anyone would be doing on deck at this time.

There was a soft, hissing whisper that he couldn't make out and he remained without moving, in the protective shadows. He could discern a darkened figure now, moving stealthily in his direction. Then the figure turned sideways and he relaxed as he saw the profile. The rounded buttocks, the high breasts, pressing against the confining cloth that covered them.

He laughed at his cautiousness. He hoped to hell he would never see the day that he would have to be afraid of anything as luscious as that.

"John, is that you?" She braced herself against the cabin wall and frowned into the darkness.

Instead of answering, he reached out and grabbed her by the waist, pulling her hard against his body. She struggled at first. Then, realizing who it was, quit fighting and responded warmly, pressing her body against his until they could have gotten into the same pair of pants. It would have been fun to try anyway.

She pushed herself away after a moment, gasping as she sucked air into her lungs. "My God! You gave me a start at first. I thought maybe it was someone else. I could just see myself flat on my back on deck with someone raping me."

"That might still happen, you know," and he smiled at her through the night.

"Oh my! I rape so easily, too." She was taunting him again. She had drawn her face back, but her lower body was still pressed tightly against him and she rubbed it from side to side teasingly. "I rape so easily," she repeated.

"Not here," he said. "Splinters, you know. Very uncomfortable, I imagine."

"My," she purred. "How nice of you. Always thinking of my little behind."

She wiggled it for emphasis and Darrow pushed her away, fearful of turning into a two-hundred-and-ten-pound quivering blob of nothing. "I was really thinking of my knees," he said. "They're rather delicate, you know."

She laughed. "I know better. There's nothing delicate in your whole big, wonderful, desirable body." She growled playfully through closed teeth and moved in on him again, her body squirming like a playful puppy.

This time, Darrow held his ground. "A coward dies a thousand deaths," he said. He repeated it again and again to himself as he gathered her into his arms.

One thing about John Darrow, he was no coward. He would have to take time before morning to pick the splinters out of his knees....

She left him just before twelve and Darrow checked the desk carefully for any telltale signs. There were none and he went below presently to awaken Apiki for the twelve o'clock watch.

Apiki came on deck a half hour later, a cup of piping hot coffee in his hand.

Darrow cautioned him on staying alert and left instructions to wake O'Mally at three o'clock. Then, after bumming a swallow of the other man's coffee, he went below.

He hesitated as he passed Elizabeth's door, then continued on to his own room. He would have to be rested if he was going to start diving in the morning.

He slid open his door and he was half way into the room, when he reconsidered. Hell, he could always sleep. He backed out and closed it softly, then turned and started back down the passageway.

Her room was dark when he entered, but he could hear her moving around on the bed. He closed the door behind him and started for the bunk.

She must have been half way expecting him because her faint whisper came through the darkness and reached his ears. "Over here, John. Hurry!"

"Hurry" wasn't the word for it. Maybe "zoom" would have been more expressive.

"No splinters here," she said as she stretched out her arms to greet him.

He sank into the bunk beside her. "That's right," he replied. "No splinters." There were two people aboard the *Malacca Maid* that night that never even thought of gold. There are a few things more important. Maybe just one thing.

CHAPTER NINETEEN

It was three o'clock before John Darrow returned to his own cabin.

The next morning he didn't awaken until after six o'clock. The sun beamed in brightly through the open porthole and played on his face, setting his brain into sluggish motion. He rolled away from it sleepily and checked his watch.

He swore when he saw the time and, rolling back over, slid his feet to the deck. He felt as much like diving as he did committing Hari-Kari, but it was his own damn fault. "You'd think a person would have better sense after thirty-four years," he thought. "Oh well, what the hell!"

He moved into the head and turned the cold water on full force in the shower. He stayed under it for twenty minutes before exiting still far from ready for the job ahead. It would have been so damn nice to go back to bed.

He shaved, brushed his teeth and slipped into a fresh pair of white ducks before going on deck. He groaned when he saw that he was the last one to arrive.

Bart Adams was taking a fix on the sun and Apiki and O'Mally had hauled the air compressor to the bow and were bolting it to the deck. Vargas came up from the hold, his arms filled with SCUBA gear, his mouth sprouting a fresh cigar. Elizabeth McClain was leaning over the starboard rail peering into the depths eagerly, as if she expected to be able to sight the *Mary Owen* from the surface.

Adams grinned at him slyly and Darrow glowered at the deck. The damned old fox could always tell when he'd been up to something ... or into someone.

He watched over Adams' shoulder as the first mate jotted down the final figures necessary to plot their position. They were about eight miles too far northeast from where he wanted to start the search pattern.

He marked an imaginary "X" on the chart with his finger and said to Adams, "Here's where we want to start. Might as well turn the engines over."

Adams saluted mockingly, the grin still spread all over his grizzled face as he disappeared through the hatch.

The engines roared to life a few seconds later and Darrow shoved the throttle to all ahead two-thirds. The spray shot up from the bow and deposited a thin film of salt water over the deck of the *Malacca Maid* as they shot forward.

Darrow stayed at the helm and they continued on that course for perhaps fifteen minutes before Adams tapped him on the shoulder, "Something off the port bow, Skipper. Could be another ship." He pointed out a dark speck on the horizon.

Darrow swore under his breath and grabbed for the binoculars. "Take the wheel, Bart. I'm going to have a look." He leaped the rail in front of the helm and was at the base of the mizzen mast in two steps. Ten seconds more and he was wrapped around the peak.

They had all seen it by this time and when Darrow looked down, he could see everyone, with the exception of Adams, gathered along the bow rail. They all must have had one word running through their minds. Hayama!

He wrapped one arm around the mast and with his free hand, raised the binoculars to his eyes. He studied the object for several seconds, watching intently as it gradually grew nearer. Presently, he climbed down from his perch, a puzzled expression covering his face.

He didn't know what to make of it.

"Well, is it Hayama?" Adams asked. His face as puzzled as Darrow's.

"No, not Hayama." He hung the glasses back on their hook.

"It's an island, Bart. A small island. Most likely an atoll from what I could see."

Adams relaxed. "So why the puzzled look? What's so strange about an atoll?"

Everyone had gathered around anxiously now and Darrow raised his voice so that all might hear. "Like I told Bart, folks, I think that's an atoll up ahead. Here's the bad part of it. Could be bad anyway. The charts make no mention of an atoll at this position. Elizabeth's father never mentioned it. What's more, if it had been there at the time the *Mary Owen* was sunk, there would most likely have been more survivors. It must have sprouted up within the last fifteen or sixteen years." He fumbled for a cigarette and lighted it.

Elizabeth pressed forward eagerly. "So what if it is an atoll. That happens all the time. They spring up all over the Pacific, everyone knows that."

"So they do. The trouble is this one sprung up here, where the *Mary Owen* went down. It's just a small ring of coral above the water, but beneath the surface it's mammoth. Gigantic! It has opened up cracks in the ocean floor and spilled lava for miles around, if it's anything like the others I've seen. The *Mary Owen* could have been swallowed up by the earth very easily."

A blanket of gloom spread like grim death over the

faces of those around him. They looked like five brides left waiting on the steps of the church.

Vargas spoke first, his voice threatening to break. "What are our chances to find her now that this has happened?"

"If they were a hundred to one before, they're a thousand to one now. Maybe more. I can tell better once I take a look at the bottom. Mr. Adams, bring her around and drop the hook about a hundred yards northeast of the atoll. I'm going down and have a look around. Apiki, start the compressor and charge one set of tanks."

It was a shattering blow to morale. Darrow's last few words had accomplished something that Suto Hayama and a hundred of his cutthroats had failed to do. For the first time since the voyage had begun, a general attitude of hopelessness prevailed.

Darrow climbed out of his white ducks and stood staring thoughtfully at the atoll for a moment. Then, his initial exploratory dive mapped out in his mind, he began to crawl into the neoprene wet suit.

The *Malacca Maid* glided to a halt and the anchor chain rattled loudly as the First Mate released the sea anchor.

No one spoke as Darrow finished donning the diving gear. Elizabeth watched him anxiously and puffed nervously on a short stub of cigarette that threatened to burn her fingers.

Vargas chewed vigorously on a dead cigar butt and stared into the water, removing the butt every few minutes to spit angrily over the side.

It was almost eight o'clock by this time and from all

outward appearances, the day was going to be a hot one. The sun, half way up in the morning sky, beamed down unmercifully, shining off of the almost still water in a dazzling brilliance that forced one to squint into the glare at all times.

The sea, perhaps thirty feet deep at this point, was clear as glass and on the bottom, green vegetation waved in and out among the masses of pink coral.

The SCUBA tanks were filled and Adams helped him on with them, at the same time making a last-minute check and adjustment of all equipment.

Darrow stepped to the rail and then turned with his back to it. He waved briefly at the onlookers, adjusted the breathing tube and face mask, and dropped backwards over the rail.

The water was cool, refreshing and beautiful. Darrow turned on his belly and glided easily along at about five feet above the ocean floor. The feeling of freedom and weightlessness was electrifying; it always was.

To Darrow, diving could never be considered work. Even while waiting at the long and monotonous decompression stops after a deep dive, he would never be bored. There was always something happening. He was a stranger in a world where, more surely than on earth, the weak shall perish and the strong shall survive. Every creature in the depths lived constantly in a world of danger, one minute the hunter, the next minute the hunted. The world on the surface was a fascinating one to be sure, but it could never be compared to the secret, eternal struggle that existed twenty-four hours a day beneath the surface.

The pink coral rose in jagged, unrealistic mountains

from the ocean floor and Darrow darted in and out among these mountains, scattering the small fish before him, arousing the curiosity of the larger ones and trying not to stir anger in those that could do him harm.

He swam outward, away from the atoll for several minutes, marveling at the unbelievable force that must have torn and ripped without mercy at the ocean floor.

At one point, about nine hundred yards from the atoll, the bottom of the sea dropped off in a dark, possibly infinite crevasse that stretched from north to south. He swam along the near rim for several hundred yards in both directions without finding any sign of a lessening. Then he returned to his original course and started across it, peering down blindly into the depths.

It was a good hundred yards before he reached the far bank. By this time, he was at about twenty fathoms and the temperature of the water was noticeably cooler where it touched his exposed skin. There had been no sign of the *Mary Owen*, but then, that would have been too much to expect. He knew but one thing for certain. If she was, by chance, at the bottom of the crevasse he had just passed, that was where she would spend eternity, gold and all.

He explored for an hour before turning back toward the ship. The next phase would be to circle the atoll.

It was an irregular, oval shape, perhaps five hundred yards long and two hundred yards across. On the side farthest away from the *Malacca Maid* he found a narrow channel leading into the center of the oval.

He swam through it slowly, measuring in his mind the varying depths and width. The *Malacca Maid* would have no trouble entering if they wanted to.

Once through the channel, the floor dropped away into bottomless depths. The very heart of the volcano, at one time a seething, boiling mass of terror.

He checked his watch. Sufficient time had passed since he left the twenty-fathom mark that he could surface without fear of the bends. He kicked upward and broke water just off of shore. A short swim and he was resting easily on the beach.

Around him the ring of coral that just barely protruded above the waves was covered here and there with a short, maybe four-foot growth of vegetation. At one point, near the southern end of the oval, a number of trees had taken root and now reached upward to the sky in a thickly populated cluster.

Unbuckling the flippers and tank, he deposited them in a neat pile well in from the water and started in a leisurely stroll along the rocky beach. The encircling rim varied in width from ten to about sixty feet and as he walked, small flocks of gulls took flight before him, screeching angrily at the intruder.

He reached the grove of palm trees and found to his satisfaction that the atoll at that point, was sandy and fairly level. With a little work, it could be made into an ideal campsite and basis of operations. As long as it was not necessary, it would be foolish to remain in the cramped quarters that the *Malacca Maid* offered.

Walking back to a point nearest the ship, he cupped his hands and called over the water. "Ahoy, the *Maid*.

Ahoy, there!"

Adams approached the near rail and waved. "Ahoy, the atoll. What's up, Skipper?"

"Bring her around to the southwest side. There's a channel where you can bring her into the cove. Plenty of room to navigate." He waved his arm for emphasis. Once they came ashore, they would make the decision about continuing the search.

He sauntered back to the grove and climbed out of the wet suit, then walked to the cove and waited on the beach for the Malacca Maid to come in.

They set up a makeshift camp in the grove that night and Darrow put off all questions about the feasibility of continuing the search until after they had eaten.

It was a light meal, but delectable, and Darrow gulped it down hungrily, topping it off with two cups of steaming hot coffee and later, a straight shot of the best bourbon he could rustle up.

They gathered around the fire a little after dark, waiting for him to speak.

He poked at the fire with a short twig, watching the short fingers of flame leap playfully back and forth for several minutes before he cleared his throat and started to speak. "Well, Elizabeth, you've footed the bill for this expedition so far, so I'm going to address my remarks to you and I want you to know that the final decision will be left entirely up to you. I'll not attempt to influence you in any way." He paused and cleared his throat again. The swim that morning had clogged his sinuses more than usual.

"To begin with, the upheaval below the surface is as

bad, if not worse, than I figured. There is a good chance that the hulk of the *Mary Owen* is completely buried beneath the tons of lava. Of course, if it is, you know as well as I do, that we're out of luck." He paused again for emphasis.

"On the other hand, the volcano has helped us to some extent. The lava has filled in about half of our search pattern to the point where the ocean is only twenty to thirty fathoms deep. In this area, we can use two divers and scour the bottom in two weeks or less. Twice as fast as we figured."

Elizabeth cut in, "I don't understand, John. If this area has been filled in, what's the use of going over it?" She sipped on the coffee she had been holding.

"That's a good question and the answer is, we can't afford not to. The ship could be in there and have been missed by the flow or it may not have been covered entirely. We may find the tip of a mast or maybe even one of her cabins jutting up above the lava. We'll have to look."

He tossed the twig all the way into the fire and did some rapid calculating in his head. "The rest of the area we can cover in about three weeks. I'll have to search that part myself." He paused again. "That's the story, what do you say? Do we go on?"

She thought for a moment before answering, her forehead wrinkled in an uncertain frown. She picked up a loose piece of coral and tossed it absently into the water after first fondling it for a moment. Suddenly, her mind made up, she got to her feet. "I've paid you for three more weeks, John. We'll look until that's used up and then we'll call it quits for good."

"The money's not the point. I think what we have to consider is the fact that Hayama is still in the picture. Every second we sit here increases his chances of finding us. If he doesn't have us pinpointed already, that is."

"Yes, I guess you're right, there." She tossed the last of the coffee into the fire. "In that case, I can't make the decision myself. We'll have to put it to a vote. I'll go along with the majority."

Darrow fumbled for a cigarette, found one and placed it in his mouth. He picked up a nearby splinter and shoved it into the fire, touching it to his cigarette when it caught fire. "All right, we'll vote on it. I think it should be a secret ballot." He removed his cap and set it on the ground at his side.

"Bart, give me a handful of your wooden matches." He extended his hand, waiting. He took the matches and sorted out five of them, giving one to each man, including himself, and passing up Elizabeth. She had already committed herself to going along with the majority vote.

"There will be only one change," he said. "If the vote is for staying, we stay until we have either covered the whole area or we run out of supplies. If the weather's good, five weeks will do it. If not, it may take two months!"

He passed the hat to Adams. "Bart, cover your hand with the cap so that we can't see. Drop the match in whole if you want to stay, broken if you think we should give up. We'll let Elizabeth count the votes."

The cap went slowly around the ring, each man hesitating before casting his vote. It came back to

Darrow, he dropped in his match and handed the cap to Elizabeth.

She pulled out the matches one at a time so that all could see. There was only one broken. She handed the cap back to Darrow. "I guess we stay," she said.

Darrow grinned as he received the cap and placed it back on his head. He puffed deeply on the cigarette. "All right, that does it. We start diving first thing in the morning. Bart, you and I will make the dive. We won't be needing the ship for the first couple of days, so both O'Mally and Apiki can remain here and start building the camp. We might as well be as comfortable as possible while we can, so take your time and do a good job."

Adams got to his feet. "What do you say, Skipper? I think this calls for a drink. I have a bottle of good scotch that I've been saving for an occasion just like this!"

No other suggestion could have been so appropriate!

CHAPTER TWENTY

The morning sun broke bright and clear over the western horizon and as the island birds first began to flutter about in the trees, Darrow and Adams stepped into the water. The search was underway.

After ten days of steady diving, there was still no sign of the *Mary Owen*. They had started at the most southerly tip of the pattern and worked methodically in a northerly direction, covering perhaps forty-five percent of the total area.

There was beginning to be some doubt as to the possible success of the search. Even Elizabeth was beginning to show signs of the strain.

On the morning of the eleventh day, they started earlier than usual. The sky was still totally dark by the time breakfast was over, and only Elizabeth, Darrow and Adams had bothered to get up for the morning meal.

Darrow sipped his coffee slowly and studied the chart before him intently. They had covered a good strip along each side of the crevasse up to this point, but had not as yet investigated its depths. Today would be the day for that.

"Bart," he said. "You stay on the beach this morning. At nine o'clock, take the dingy out and bring me down a fresh set of tanks. You'll have to dive without oxygen, so I'll meet you at the five-fathom level. With the fresh tanks, I can stay down for perhaps another hour. I can maybe have half of it covered by the time I have to come up."

"Right-o, Skipper. How deep you going to go?" Adams sat across the fire from him, sipping gingerly on a tin cup full of black coffee and puffing on the charred pipe.

"Could be that I'll have to go fifty fathoms or better. If that's the case, most of my diving time will be spent at the decompression stops. I can only stay at that level for an hour, maybe seventy-five minutes at the most. If we change tanks at the five-fathom level, I can maybe sit there a while and then go back down." He sipped again on the coffee and fumbled for a cigarette.

"You'll have to bring down another set of tanks at one thirty this afternoon. I'll meet you at the same spot. I'm cutting it close, so for God's sake don't be late."

Adams rose to his feet and threw the last of his coffee on the fire. "I'll be there. Just see that you are. O' course, if you're not, I might take over the *Maid* and head for Tahiti. I remember I was there once before the war. Gals don't wear many clothes down there. Least they didn't at that time. I figure it'd be the best damn place in the world for old Bart to retire." He grinned wryly and stuffed the pipe in his pocket, wiggling his hips in the popular conception of a Tahitian dancer. "Yes sir, old Bart could have a ball down there!"

"Old Bart, as you put it, would kill himself in about a week, or I miss my guess."

Adams grinned again, "Listen, Skipper. What you young fellas don't realize is that by the time you get my age, you start shoppin' around for ways you'd like to go. You figure you got maybe ten, fifteen years. But then that isn't really much time at all. It goes fast. Real fast." He spit into the fire and wiped his mouth with the back of a grimy sleeve. "Well," he continued, "you start shoppin' around. I've done my shoppin' and that's the way I want it to come. I'll find me three or four o' them bare-breasted Tahitian mamas and I'll hole up in some little shack back up in the hills and that's where I'll stay. Then one day there'll be a procession comin' down off of the mountain. The women'll be moanin' and wailin' and they'll be packin' ol' Bart and he'll be deader than a door nail, but you know what? He won't have no pants on, he'll have the old pipe here in one fist and he'll be grinnin' from ear to ear. Then they'll put up an old wood stake and it'll say:

Here lies old Bart Adams,
A friend of all whores and madams;
A happier corpse you never will see,
'Cause he didn't die from lack-a-nooki!

Adams finished the eulogy, still grinning, and sat down again.

Darrow laughed and finished his coffee. He glanced at Elizabeth and she didn't know whether to grin or not. She most likely thought he was just shooting off his mouth, but Darrow knew better. He knew damn well that Bart knew how to live. It was like him to have it all figured out how he was going to die.

A half hour later he and Adams dropped anchor from the dinghy and Darrow made a last-minute check of his equipment. He glanced at the shoreline and estimated that they were about a half mile out from the atoll. "O.K. Bart. I'll see you here at nine o'clock and again at one-thirty. For Christ's sake be on time."

"Right, Skipper. I'll be here. Good hunting." He shook hands for luck and then watched as Darrow dropped backwards into the water and sank out of sight.

The sky was overcast on this day and there was a stiff breeze whipping the whitecaps into motion. Beneath the surface, there was little light and by the time Darrow reached sixty feet, he was forced to switch on the lantern.

He hit the crevasse at the southern border of the search pattern and started north along its eastern side, sweeping the lantern before him as he swam.

On this pass, he would keep about twenty feet below the rim of the crevasse. On the way back, sixty feet below the rim. Then he would do the same on the opposite side.

It would have been easy if he could have confined the search to only an object the size of the *Mary Owen*, but that was not practical. When he finally found her, if he ever did, it would most likely be as a result of following a slim trail to her grave. An anchor here, part of a rail there, maybe a cabin door half buried in the mud or lava.

As he swam, he saw that the walls of the crevasse were as he had expected them to be. Not sheer cliffs, but jagged, twisting slopes with cracks and ledges that could easily bear the weight of the dead bulk of the *Mary Owen*. They could not afford to overlook the fact that she had been pushed into the crevasse and hung up before she went all the way to the bottom. When the stakes were twelve million beautiful bucks, you didn't overlook a damn thing.

An odd-looking object protruded from the mud of a ledge a few feet below him and he kicked down eagerly for a look, a moment of excitement starting his heart beating rapidly and increasing his rhythmic breathing to the point where it used up precious pounds of the canned oxygen.

He swam around it for a few seconds, then took his knife and chipped away the barnacles and marine growth that covered its exposed surface. He realized suddenly what it was and kicked away. "Poor bastards," he thought. It was the tail section of a large plane. Most likely a B-17 that had gone down during the Pacific War. If there had been anyone inside, they might as well rest in peace.

He floated back up to his original course and continued on down the trench until he reached what he estimated would be the northernmost edge of the search pattern. Then he reversed his direction and started back, dropping another forty feet or so deeper.

By nine o'clock, he had covered the eastern wall from one end to the other and as deep as it was possible for him to go with the air supply he had.

He completed the rendezvous with Bart Adams and switched SCUBA tanks at exactly nine o'clock. After that, he rested a while, then dropped back down and crossed to the western wall of the trench for the second half of the run.

Two hours later, he had gone all the way north, dropped down the forty feet and was half way through with the return trip. That's when he spotted it. A broken section of mast that protruded only a few feet out of the mud.

It was unmistakable, it couldn't be anything else. He swam around it several times and then darted quickly back and forth along each side of it.

There was nothing else, just the mast. It could have been from any one of a thousand ships he told himself. There was no need to get excited and build himself up for a big letdown. Deep in his heart, though, he was sure it was from the *Mary Owen*. He knew it was. It had to be. It had to.

CHAPTER TWENTY-ONE

He swam closer and chipped away at it with his knife. From what he knew of marine biology, the growth that covered it to a depth of an inch or better would have taken about sixteen or seventeen years to form. At least the time element was right. Everything was right. Everything!

He started deeper along the slope, a sweeping zigzag type dive that spanned a width of maybe twenty feet. He had to move slowly, pausing to inspect every mound, every hole that he passed. Each time he stopped, his hands shook as he chipped at the barnacles.

He continued down, deeper, deeper. The depth gauge read thirty, thirty-five, then forty fathoms. He checked his air supply and it was dangerously low.

At forty-one fathoms, he found the chain. An anchor chain, most likely torn away as the *Mary Owen* plunged down the side of the crevasse. He followed it downward excitedly, pulling himself along it and cutting his hands painfully on the sharp growth. It disappeared into the mud in only ten feet.

He was growing lightheaded by this time, partly from the excitement and partly from the depth. This was dangerous and he fought to clear his head.

It was at fifty fathoms, three hundred feet, that he first saw the other mast. This time, it wasn't torn loose, though. It was attached to a deck. The battered, barnacle covered deck of the *Mary Owen*!

He wanted to dance, to shout. He wanted to scream to the world that he had found her. He was rich beyond his wildest dreams. They all were.

He backed off a bit to better survey the entire situation. The *Mary Owen* was sticking bow first into the bank. There were perhaps fifty feet of the stern that had not been buried and she was right side up.

The interior of the ship had undoubtedly been flooded. That would equalize the pressure, inside and out. Therefore, the tons of lava and mud that had cascaded down over her bow would not have crushed her. He had it figured out in no time at all. Cut a hole in the stern with a torch and the gold was theirs for the taking. It was as easy as eating apple pie.

He tied a line quickly to the mast and released the marker buoy, then he started back up to keep the rendezvous with Adams. He looked at his watch and he would be fifteen minutes late, but what the hell. A rich bastard like John Darrow could keep an army waiting for something as important as this.

He didn't figure that Bart Adams would mind when he gave him the news!

Darrow reached the thirty-foot level after several decompression stops, consuming an hour's time. Above him, he could see the bottom of the dingy rocking gently in the swells.

He blew a few air bubbles to the surface as the signal for Adams to bring down the spare tank and then, while he waited, scribbled a hasty message on his slate and unbuckled it from his leg. He wished he could be on the surface to see the expression on their faces when they read it.

He had written just one word, "JACKPOT!" That would be enough.

Overhead he heard the splash and saw the foamy explosion as Adams hit the water.

They switched tanks in a matter of a few seconds and the First Mate struck out again for the surface, taking the used tanks and the slate. Darrow would have dared to state that Shakespeare never wrote a word or even a whole chapter that caused more comment.

Before long he began to feel the sharp pains in his joints and lungs and he realized that he had surfaced too rapidly. A slight case of the bends.

He dropped back down to sixty feet and the pain subsided. He would have to stay there for an hour and a half at least before surfacing.

The wait was long and boring. Instead of an hour and a half, it seemed like days. Time and time again he had to fight down an overpowering urge to go up ahead of time, bends or no bends. Like all things, however, the time passed and he reached the surface not a second later than possible.

Bart Adams sat patiently in the dingy and when he saw Darrow; he removed the pipe from his mouth just long enough to grin happily. Then he plopped it back in and pulled Darrow over the stern of the little craft.

Strangely enough, now that Darrow had surfaced, now that he could cut loose with all of his elation, the initial excitement had vanished. Once more, he was just a man with a job to do. He spit the breathing tube from his mouth and reflected that oddly enough, he felt no different. Damn it all, he still put his pants on one leg at a time.

"Well, Bart, old boy. We made it! We finally hit it big." He grinned and gripped the First Mate's hand in a hearty shake of congratulations.

Adams picked up the oars and began to pull toward shore. "So, we did Skipper, so we did. For some reason or other, though, I'm not real happy. For the first time since this damn mess started, I realized that I'm not a bit more satisfied than when I was First Mate o' the *Malacca Maid*. I guess we're all rich now, but I'm richer than any o' you bastards. It took money to make me realize that I had everything I wanted just bein' your First Mate."

He pulled hard on the oars and sucked loudly on the pipe that had long since gone out. "I guess that's all over now, though. All any of us have left is money. I guess me and the *Maid* will go into dry dock together."

"Don't be a damn fool," Darrow grinned. "Neither you or the *Maid* is going to be beached. I've been thinking, Bart. This organization needs two ships. Maybe, three. Then we could really start to trade. We might not have the biggest trading company in the Orient, but by God, we'll have the best. I figure I'll need a partner and another Skipper. I'm looking at both of them right now. That is, if you're interested."

"Interested! Why you young son of a bitch. You know damn well I am." Adams let the oars sway loosely in their locks and the two men gripped each other's hands. "To the best damned trading company in the Far East!"

Adams began to pull the oars again and Darrow

laughed as he unstrapped the SCUBA gear from his back and climbed out of the wet suit. "I was just thinking. Wouldn't it be something if that story about the gold had been nothing more than a sea story from the beginning." He took a cigarette from a pack in the bottom the dingy and struck a match to it. "We still haven't seen the gold."

Adams shrugged his shoulders. "Then we'd still have the *Malacca Maid*. We'd have to settle for the second-best trading company in the Far East."

"I guess you're right. What's so damn bad about that?"

They were just a hundred yards or so from shore by this time and the others could be seen milling around impatiently on the beach. Elizabeth yelled something and waved a handkerchief. When they landed, she rushed forward and Darrow took her in his arms. She was trembling with excitement.

Around them there was yelling, crying and dancing, but Darrow and Elizabeth said nothing. Their eyes told each other all that either needed to know.

CHAPTER TWENTY-TWO

That night, Darrow got drunk. Ass over tea kettle, staggering drunk. He hadn't pitched one since the night he met Elizabeth, but this night he made up for it.

They built a fire in the center of camp and broke out the bottles. For two or three hours, there was chaos. Utter chaos. Bart Adams ended up by doing a

Hawaiian War Dance with Apiki and then collapsed at the end. He was saved by O'Mally from rolling into the fire. Apiki decided at midnight that he was going to walk barefooted through the glowing coals like his ancestors had done and Darrow had to put him to sleep with a tap on the jaw.

When all had quieted down, Darrow and Elizabeth took a walk to the end of the atoll. The shifting beach sand was cool under their bare feet and from time to time, a sea crab would scurry awkwardly away from them in a strange, sideways motion. A gull took flight before them with a shrill screech of surprise.

Overhead the sky was clear and between the large, South Sea moon and the twinkling stars, the night was illuminated almost to the point of broad daylight.

At the far end of the atoll, the Masabate grass grew thickly to a height of six feet or better and Darrow reached out for her hand as he led her through.

They stopped at a large rock that was the highest point on the atoll and Darrow helped her to its peak. Thirty feet below them, the ocean crashed with a deep roar against the rocky shore line, filling the air with a fine spray.

Elizabeth sat cross-legged on the flat peak of the rock and pulled Darrow down beside her. "Well, John, I'll bet when we started, you never thought it could be done."

He pulled his cigarettes from his shirt pocket and handed her one, took one himself and then lighted them both before answering. "I've seen too many of these things, Elizabeth. I've seen people that spend a lifetime searching for something that wasn't anywhere close to being this big. I've seen good men kill, die of frustration and despair, or just plain go to ruin, tracking down a tale that was maybe a hundred, even two hundred years old. Treasures, or mythical treasures that would total no more than fifty thousand dollars."

He puffed on the cigarette and stared out over the water. "When you came to me with this, it was just another job. The story sounded plausible, but the chances of success were so small, that I never dreamed it could be done. Oh, I got swept up with the fever all right. I was just as gold hungry as anyone; but deep down inside, I kept telling myself that it was just another wild goose chase. I guess it was mental insurance against failure."

She smiled and moved closer to him, resting her head on his shoulder. "I think we've found something more precious than gold, though. At least, I have. That night on the *Malacca Maid* I told you I wasn't sure how I felt. I said it may have been just a physical attraction, remember?"

Darrow squirmed uneasily, debating whether or not to change the subject. "Sure," he said. "You don't expect me to forget that do you?"

"No, no I don't. I would have been damn hurt, if you had. It's more than physical with me, John. I know that now. I don't know how you feel. I'm half afraid to think about it." She fondled his hand absently.

Darrow puffed hard on the cigarette and evaded her eyes, not knowing how to answer. Not knowing what to answer, unsure of his own emotions. Finally he said, "There has been so much happening, so many things to think about. Frankly, I'm still not sure how

I feel. I wish I could tell you, one way or the other."

She took his face in her fingers and turned his eyes to her. She kissed him softly on the lips and then drew back. "I shouldn't have asked. It could have been worse, though. You could have said it was just another affair that would end when we returned to Macao. You didn't, though, and that means I still have a chance."

She stretched her legs out on the rock and drew him down on top of her.

Darrow's hand caressed her leg where the cloth of her shorts ended. He felt her arms tighten around his neck and he fumbled with her zipper.

"Not here," she said. "We're silhouetted against the sky. If anyone happened to look this way ..."

He helped her to her feet and they scrambled down the rock and into the Masabate grass. There was a small clearing in the center of the grass and they sank to the ground.

"This is better," she said. "Much better." She slipped out of the shorts unaided. He leaped to her, pressing his lips against her neck, breasts, all the way down to her ankles. He squeezed her calves and caressed them hard with his mouth, almost biting her. She moved suddenly, whispered, "Oh, John, John, more, more, more ..."

But Darrow wasn't listening. He didn't have to. It was a long time before his lips met hers again, but when they did, Elizabeth could only hear the sound of her own tumultuous heartbeat and feel the tide of her passion rippling across her body in a growing tidal wave.

CHAPTER TWENTY-THREE

By dawn, they had boarded the *Malacca Maid* for the first time in several days and had dropped the sea anchor at a spot alongside the bobbing marker buoy.

They would use two divers for the recovery of the gold. Adams, in the deep-sea rig that was fed from the pump on the surface and Darrow, who would dive in the SCUBA gear. By working this way, Darrow would have the advantage of freedom of movement and Adams would be able to spend much more time on the bottom.

The sun rose at five thirty-five, and two minutes later they lowered Adams into the water. He would make the initial dive and with the cutting torch, open a hole in the stern of the *Mary Owen*. When this was done, Darrow would go down and enter the ship in an effort to locate the crates that held the gold.

Darrow watched intently as the winch lowered Adams into the water. Once under the surface, he was released and slowly drifted downward out of sight.

Darrow picked up the diving phone and spoke into it. "Bart, this is Captain Darrow. Can you hear me?"

"I hear you loud and clear, Skipper. I'm following the line from the marker buoy and I'm down about ten fathoms already. Everything working O.K."

"That's fine, Bart. That suit you have there is ten years older than God, so give me a progress report every ten fathoms till you reach the wreck."

"Roger, Skipper. I'm at fifteen fathoms now. So far, so good."

Darrow handed the phone to Apiki and lighted a cigarette nervously. "He's too damn old to be diving," he thought. "The trouble is it's a two-man job down there and neither Apiki or O'Mally may have the experience to make the dive."

He flipped the match over the rail and puffed hard on the cigarette, his eyes constantly watching the life line and air line, as they unreeled from the winch. It was moving too fast and he geared the motor down another notch for safety's sake.

He could hear the very faint crackle from the phone as Adams continued to send up his depth reports. Darrow crossed his fingers and waited. He had been a damn fool not to buy a new diving rig before they left Macao.

A second later, Apiki reached over and switched off the winch. "He's on the deck of the *Mary Owen*, Skipper. Says he's going to look around a bit before he starts cutting." Apiki handed the phone back to Darrow.

"This is Darrow again, Bart. For God's sake don't foul your lines. Those barnacles are razor sharp!"

"Goddamn it, Skipper. Don't you think I ever made a dive before? I just want to check around before I go to work with the torch."

There was a moment's pause and then, "Skipper, ask Miss McClain if she knows what hold the stuff is in. I think the easiest thing would be to cut right through the deck."

Darrow asked and Elizabeth shook her head. He

spoke into the phone again. "The answer is no, Bart. Look before you start cutting see if there isn't a hatch that wasn't buried. No sense in cutting, if we don't have to."

"Already checked that. All hold covers were buried, but the hatchway to the crew's quarters is out in the open. Won't open, though. It's solid steel and I figure the ship twisted some and she jammed. We'd have to blast it off if we wanted it open. I think it's easier to cut our way through."

"Right-o. Use your own judgment. If you need any help, just give a yell and I'll come down. If not, I'll be down as soon as you get through with the torch."

Adams acknowledged and Darrow returned the phone to Apiki. "O'Mally, send down the acetylene tanks and the torch. He's ready to cut." He lighted a second cigarette from the butt of the first and moved back to watch the overall operations. Time passed too damn slow on deck. He wished to hell he could be down below, where he knew what was going on.

The welding equipment went down and Darrow moved to the rail where he could watch the air bubbles from the working diver.

The sun was beating down warmly by this time and he removed his jacket, throwing it on the deck behind the air compressor. If all went well, Adams should be able to cut through in about three hours. After that, they could really go to work.

He realized suddenly that they had grown lax in their security measures.

Vargas leaned against the rail further down. He was smoking heavily on a fresh cigar and dabbing at his sweated face and throat with a red handkerchief.

Darrow picked up the binoculars from their place by the helm and gave them to Vargas. "Climb the mizzenmast and keep a sharp eye out in all directions with these. It's going to be hot and tiresome, but I'm afraid I won't be able to relieve you. We'll need all hands to man the diving rig."

Vargas shifted the cigar to the side of his mouth with a rolling motion of his tongue and pocketed the handkerchief. "All right, Captain. Seems to me that we could watch right from the deck, though. Must be ten miles to the horizons. I'm a little old to be climbing that damn mast."

"Sorry, Vargas. We can't afford to be caught by Hayama with a man on the bottom. If something does happen, we'll need every available second to bring him up."

"I see. Well, perhaps there will be a little more breeze up there." He dropped the binocular strap over his neck and headed for the mast.

Elizabeth came over and placed a hand on Darrow's arm. "I feel rather useless. Do you suppose anyone would like coffee?"

"You can ask around. As for me, it's too damn hot for coffee. Thanks, anyway." He took her hand and squeezed it reassuringly. "You might make some ice tea." He didn't really want any, but it would give her something to do.

"Good idea. I'm going below, but let me know if anything happens." She left him and disappeared through the hatch. When she had gone, he breathed easier. After their conversation of last night, he felt guilty. He had taken advantage of her for no reason other than animal lust. Of course, it took "two to tango" and it wasn't as though she was the first. He supposed that the real basis for his uneasiness was his inability to return her love, other than in a physical sense.

The acetylene torch had been lowered by this time and Darrow took the phone from Apiki. "She's on her way down, Bart. Keep your head up."

"Right-o, Skipper. Head up and eyes open." There was a short pause and Darrow could hear the sound of Adams' breathing over the phone.

Suddenly it quickened and there was a brief grunt from the other end of the line. Then: "Having a little trouble regulating the pressure down here, Cap. The safety valve seems to have a leak. I almost blew myself to the surface just then. I think I have it under control now. At least for the time being."

Darrow flipped the half-smoked cigarette over the side and stared at the water as a sudden explosion of air bubbled to the surface like water in a boiling pot. Even though it seemed to be under control at the present, it could develop into a dangerous situation. The pressure in the rubber suit was regulated by the diver on the bottom. At this depth, just enough pressure was maintained to keep water out of the diving helmet. If something went wrong and the suit inflated accidentally, the diver would be shot to the surface. The least that could happen would be a bad case of the bends. The worst would be that the sudden change in pressure as the diver reached the surface would explode his lungs. Either way, it was no picnic.

"Bart, I think you had better come up now. No sense

in tempting fate."

"No dice, Skipper. I've got it under control. It should be O.K. now."

"All right, Goddamn it, but listen, if it happens again, up you come." Darrow stared at the air bubbles, his forehead wrinkled with concern.

Apiki and O'Mally stood tensely nearby, the sweat rolling from their faces. Both were aware of the consequences of such a malfunction.

Adams' voice crackled again and Darrow picked up the phone. "I've started to cut now, Skipper. The deck is a little thicker than I thought it would be, but I'm almost through in one spot. I'll keep you informed as I go along."

There was nothing to do now, but wait, the hardest job of all. The diving operations required little work, but constant vigilance from those on the surface.

Elizabeth McClain came back up with the ice tea and Darrow sipped on it slowly as he watched. It tasted pretty damn good, after all.

Three hours later, Darrow joined Adams on the deck of the *Mary Owen*. It had all been talked out beforehand. Adams would stand by the entrance hole and Darrow would enter the wreck to locate the crates of gold.

He flicked on the torch and gripping the short crowbar in his other hand, stepped down into the black hole. What he saw, wasn't very pretty.

He had dropped into the Number Three hold and it was evident that, at the time of the evacuation of Canton, the refugees had been packed into the hold like cattle. When they were torpedoed, they had no chance whatsoever to reach the deck. It must have been hell.

After all these years, there wasn't much to see. Time, water and the fish had done their work well. All that remained were bits of cloth, shredded and rotten. Now and then the rays of his lantern would pass over a grinning skull. In this one compartment there must have been, at one time, three hundred living bodies. Now, there was only the decayed remains of three hundred corpses.

He swam slowly over the rubble from one bulkhead to the other, fighting hard to keep from throwing up. For a moment, he hated the Japanese again.

He swam to the aft bulkhead and stopped at a steel door. It wouldn't budge. He brought the crowbar into play and it swung open slowly, an inch at a time. On the other side there was nothing but more corpses.

He would have to go up into the forward half of the ship. The gold must have been stored in the forward hold. That was the way his luck usually ran.

He turned and swam back across the maze of decayed corpses. He couldn't help but wonder if they knew they had been buried with twelve million dollars. Obviously, they didn't, but it was ironic. People, ninety percent of whom hadn't known from day to day where their next meal was coming from, living a life of poverty and then knowing wealth only in death. In further thought, he figured that they had found their wealth in freedom, rather than in gold.

There were two levels leading out of the hold and Darrow chose the top door in hopes that the going would be easier. Again, he had to use the crowbar on the door and when he finally pushed through, he found himself in a narrow passageway. He thought for a moment and then decided against opening any of the doors that lined the hall on each side. He had seen enough of death.

The Number Two hold was the same as the aft hold. Only corpses. All cargo must have been loaded in Number One hold. He continued forward, noting that it was a strange feeling to move along halls that had seen only death and fish for fifteen years. He shivered at the thought.

He was deep beneath the lava now and his lantern flashed on a heavy door ahead of him. That would be it. On the other side of that door, unless someone was cockeyed as hell, was twelve million dollars in solid gold bars. His for the taking.

He worked on the latches that secured the door. Two, then three came free. Two others wouldn't budge. He pounded on the door in frustration then, realizing the futileness of it all, started back in the direction of Adams. They would have to use the torch again.

He swam through the hole in the deck to find Adams resting casually on the acetylene tank. Darrow scribbled hurriedly on his slate, "Have to cut again. Need help. Signal for more line and follow."

Adams nodded agreement and tugged twice on his life line, then picked up the cutting tools.

The line grew slack as the winch started to unwind and Darrow lowered the other diver into the hole, guiding the air line carefully away from the sharp rim.

It was fifteen minutes of careful progress before they

reached the door and when they did, they began cutting immediately. In five minutes, the two latches fell free and they tried the door. It wouldn't budge.

As the ship settled, it must have twisted and jammed the door into permanent position. After all these years, it would be as solid as if it had been welded.

Darrow swore disgustedly to himself and looked at Adams who only nodded. They would have to cut through the door. At least an inch of steel.

He looked at his watch and the time was running short. Adams had been down for four hours now and Darrow had been down about thirty minutes. They would have to work fast.

Decompression time, within reason, was no problem to Adams as long as the air compressor on the *Malacca Maid* held out. With Darrow, it was another story. If he stayed down an hour and fifteen minutes, which was about maximum, he would have to spend almost five hours in decompression stops on the way up. They would have to bring him down a spare tank.

He checked his watch again and did a fast mental calculation, then scribbled on the slate, "Tell the surface to put a line over in one and a half hours with a fresh tank. I will intercept at sixty feet."

Adams nodded in the affirmative and Darrow could see his lips move as he spoke to the *Malacca Maid*. He waited a moment, then signaled that it would be done.

With that settled, they went to work on the jammed door.

The work went fast and a half hour later a thirty-six-inch circle fell out of the steel. Darrow had fifteen minutes to locate the crates of gold.

Darrow squeezed slowly through the hole and then reached back for the lantern. He flashed it ahead of him and saw to his satisfaction that the hold was jammed with cargo. If the gold were aboard, this is where it would be found.

He kicked further into the compartment and surveyed the situation. It was still going to be a hell of a job. The crates, boxes and trunks had been stacked orderly at one time, but between the torpedo and the wild shifting of the *Mary Owen*, the cargo had been scattered helter-skelter. There was no telling how much they would have to move to find the right crates. One hell of a job to say the least.

It was in this part of the ship that she had taken the torpedo, too. On the port side, at what once had been the water line, a gaping hole had been ripped into the hull, the jagged steel twisting grotesquely inward. Lava and mud had poured through the hole by the ton during the volcano eruption.

The smaller crates he could move by hand, others, he would have to rig a block and tackle to move. It was foolish in what little time he had left, but he began methodically shifting crates out of the one corner. The urge was so great by this time that he felt he couldn't waste a moment.

He was almost to the bottom in that one spot, when he saw it. A metal bar! He couldn't be sure it was gold, because it was discolored and covered with barnacles and other undersea growth, but the chances were good! Damn good!

He removed his knife from the sheath and dug at

the bar shakily. It was soft. He peeled off a thin strip with the knife and the yellow metal stared up at him. He was so shaken, he could hardly think. He knew but one thing as he cradled the bar in his arms. He was holding about fifty-five thousand dollars in the form of the most easily exchangeable property in the world. Solid gold!

As near as he could estimate, it weighed close to a hundred pounds, but under water it was easy to handle. He swam to the hole and shoved it through to Adams. He started to laugh in his excitement and the mouth piece popped out. He choked on the water, then recovered and looked at Adams. Through the face plate, white teeth flashed as the older man grinned from ear to ear.

Adams imagined that all would be pandemonium on the surface by this time. Adams had surely passed the word over the phone.

Darrow left the hole and kicked his way back down to the corner. Just a little longer. Time be damned.

At first he could find nothing. Then he saw the other bar, half covered by a rotted steamer trunk. He pried it free and headed back for the opening. Like it or not, they would have to start the trip to the surface. Time had run out.

He shoved it through the hole and squeezed after it. He signaled to Adams that they would leave the cutting equipment where it was and take the gold. The decision was an easy one to make.

They started back down the corridor, Adams in the lead lifeline, Darrow following closely, gathering in the played-out lifeline.

It was an awkward situation, but not too dangerous if they took their time.

Because of the sharp edges on the opening that had been cut in the deck, they could not pull the lifeline and air line across it.

The only alternative was to accumulate the line on the bottom of the Number Three hold and then allow the winch on the *Malacca Maid* to pull it straight up.

The trip to Number Three hold was slow, but without incident and in thirty minutes they found themselves on the slightly tilted deck of the *Mary Owen*.

The two gold bars were sent up immediately in the basket and Darrow and Adams began the ever so slow trip to the surface.

Darrow looked at his watch. He had been at the three-hundred-foot level for two hours. More than twice as long as was recommended in the Navy Standard Decompression Table. If he didn't come down with a hell of a case of the bends after this dive, he never would.

CHAPTER TWENTY-FOUR

It was almost five in the afternoon by the time Darrow and Adams reached the deck of the *Malacca Maid*. It had been a long day. A hell of a long day and both men were exhausted. Too exhausted to share in the elation of the others.

Apiki had gone diving for abalone as soon as they returned to the atoll and the meal that night was more than delicious, but it was eaten in silence.

By that time, each person was wrapped in his own individual thoughts, each seeming to avoid any conversation with the others.

Darrow ate wearily and even though hungry, finished but half of his meal. Besides the fatigue, he kept waiting for the first signs of the bends which he felt were sure to appear.

Lady luck was with him on this trip, however, and the evening passed without so much as a symptom. By ten o'clock, he was in dead slumber.

That night he dreamed of Hayama. In his dream, he saw him as a creature with a hundred arms that reached out murderously for everyone in sight, crushing his victims to his horrible body like a giant squid.

When he awoke, his body was bathed in sweat and he stifled a scream. He dashed out of the lean-to and looked around apprehensively. On a high rock above the pounding sea, his sentry was silhouetted in black against the faint light of dawn. There was nothing else.

He relaxed and laughed at his nervousness, reassured by the fact that it had been a dream and nothing more. He was letting his imagination get the best of him.

He lighted a cigarette and walked slowly to the rock where the sentry sat. As he neared the rock, he recognized the guard as Apiki and he spoke softly so as not to alarm the man. "How's she going, fella? Anything happening?"

Apiki turned sharply and then relaxed when he saw who it was. "Everything's quiet so far, skipper." He gestured out over the water. "Not even a gull in the air."

"Let's hope it stays that way. If we can hold out for another twenty-four hours, we've got it made." Darrow puffed on the cigarette and then blew the smoke out in the direction of the sea. "Sooner or later I suppose we'll run up against Hayama, but let's hope the next time it'll be on our terms."

Apiki rubbed at his bandaged skull and nodded in agreement. "One of these days I've got a little score of my own to settle. The sooner the better." He hesitated a moment. "After we get the gold to the top, that is."

Darrow slapped him on the shoulder encouragingly and started back to the camp. He looked at his watch and then quickened his stride. It was four-thirty and they would have to pack a lot of diving into the next twelve or fourteen hours.

He routed the others out of their beds and started to build the breakfast fire. It had rained some that night and he threw gasoline on the dampened wood to get it going. After it blazed for a few minutes he put the water on for coffee and then began to outline, in his mind, the work procedure for that day.

He would leave Vargas and Elizabeth on the atoll to break up camp and gather together the remaining supplies. Adams, O'Mally, Apiki and himself would put in the *Malacca Maid* and handle the diving operations. With any luck at all, they would be through diving by late that afternoon. After that, the faster they cleared the area, the better it would be.

Elizabeth prepared a light breakfast and it was gulped down quickly. With the prospects of raising the gold that day, even the most common, everyday task seemed horribly slow and painstaking.

By five-thirty, they had dropped anchor beside the marker buoy and Darrow and Adams were making a final check of their gear in preparation for the dive. It would be carried out as it had been yesterday, Darrow free diving in the SCUBA gear and Adams in the deep-sea rig.

Darrow dropped over the side and began to follow the buoy line down slowly to the wreck. He was worried this morning, wondering if he had made the right decision in leaving Elizabeth and Vargas on shore. If Hayama did happen to stumble on them, the two men left on the deck of the Malacca Maid would have to abandon the winch and the air compressor to defend themselves. Bart Adams would be at the mercy of the depths. As good as dead, most likely.

On the other hand, it was important that they break camp and be ready to sail as soon as possible. Vargas and Elizabeth were carrying out an important phase of the operations. If at all possible, Darrow would like to get underway that evening and put as many miles between themselves and the area as possible.

He attempted to dismiss it from his mind. Not because it wasn't a vital subject, but because there was nothing he could do to correct it. He had made the decision and felt it was the correct one. Correct or not, he would have to stand behind it.

He reached the deck of the *Mary Owen* and halted to wait for Adams who landed beside him in a few seconds. Then they descended together into the wreck.

They reached the Number One hold in a few minutes

and Darrow wriggled through the small opening. He would have to work fast.

The very fact that he had stayed down so long the day before without any visible after effects had tended to encourage him, but he knew that it was foolhardy to tempt fate any more than necessary. The physical and emotional strain he had been placed under would make him more susceptible to the bends every day.

Adams began to rig a hasty block and tackle in case it was needed for the heavier crates and Darrow started in on the lighter ones, working from the corner where he had found the two bars on the preceding day.

The work went slow. Slower than hell, and by the time he had been down an hour, they had found nothing. It looked like they might have to make two dives.

He came upon a badly broken crate that contained the rusted remains of an American automobile of about the nineteen thirty-seven vintage and Darrow signaled for the block and tackle. He didn't know where the hell he would move it to, but it had to be moved. There was no getting around it.

He hooked onto the body after a few minutes of work and signaled for Adams to start pulling. The rope tightened and the car began to slowly rise from the bottom, clouding the water with a mucky silt and making it almost impossible to see.

Adams pulled and Darrow guided the car to the top of the hold and then back to a far corner where they dropped it gingerly on a pile of rotting crates. Returning to the corner, he went to work again on the lighter crates.

He checked his watch and he had been down an hour and twenty-five minutes. Time was running short. He quickened his pace, tearing almost frantically at the rubble.

Ten minutes later he found it, a battered crate almost covered by silt and debris. One side had broken open and the precious bars poured out in a jumbled heap. Behind it, he found the second crate still intact.

One by one, he transported the bars to the place where Adams waited and when they were all assembled, they began the trip back to the Number Three hold.

The basket was lowered from the *Malacca Maid* and Adams began loading the gold for the trip to the surface, five bars at a time because of the weight.

Darrow made four trips to the Number One hold before the last of the gold was brought out. Twelve million dollars had been a close guess.

Darrow had been down two hours, when the last basket started for the surface. Like a damn fool, he had pushed his luck again. Maybe, too far. He tapped Adams on the shoulder and signaled that they should start for the surface.

Rising as rapidly as it was safe to, Darrow was perhaps thirty feet above the wreck when he realized that Adams wasn't with him. It could mean but one thing. Bart was in trouble.

He mentally cursed their luck and started back down, hoping to hell it was something minor, fearing that it wasn't.

A second later his worst fears were realized.

Sometime during the past few minutes, Adams had tangled his lifeline in the twisted superstructure of the *Mary Owen* without becoming aware of it. When they had started the winch on the *Malacca Maid*, the line must have become wedged tightly in the wreckage. Now the air line was pinched dangerously, allowing only a minimum of air to get through.

He stopped at Adams' side and the man scribbled hastily on his slate. He was getting air, but the pressure was just enough to keep the water out of his helmet. If the line closed any more, he would drown in a matter of seconds.

Darrow signaled that he understood and swam hurriedly to the source of the trouble. It was bad all right. Damn bad and it didn't take a genius to see it.

He moved above the tangle and signaled the surface for more slack with two quick tugs on the line. They gave it to him and he began working feverishly on the line. Every second he wasted would bring Adams closer to death.

Suddenly he was aware that his First Mate was signaling frantically. Now what the hell could be wrong he wondered. As if they needed anything else.

When he reached Adams, the man shoved the slate at him quickly. Darrow's heart sank as he read the hastily scribbled message, "Surface reports that Hayama's junk has just been sighted. Get the hell out of here. I'll try to free myself. They'll need you on the surface."

Darrow shook his head in a negative reply. He had to stay with Adams. If they wanted to get away from Hayama, they would have to make a run for it as soon as possible. If he knew his crew, they wouldn't be about to leave with a diver on the bottom. The only chance any of them had was to free Bart. Once he was untangled, they could yank him to the surface and worry about decompressing later. It had to be this way.

He swam back to the tangled lines and tore at the rubble that pinned them with his bare hands. He couldn't move a thing. "Have to get the crowbar," he thought. "I'll never get him free this way."

He swam back to the hole that had been cut into the *Mary Owen* and started through. They had discarded the bar in the forward hold like damn fools. Now it might make the difference between life and death for Bart Adams.

It was then he looked at Bart. The First Mate was signaling wildly for Darrow to surface. He must have known that Darrow's stay under water had far exceeded the safety limits by this time and he would have to surface soon or even decompression wouldn't help him. Also, they must have been in bad trouble on the surface. It was save Adams or save himself and Darrow realized it, but he shook his head stubbornly and started on down into the wreck.

Then he saw the knife. He didn't realize what was happening at first. His brain had been fogged by the depth and he even had to fight off a sudden impulse to laugh. Nitrogen narcosis. An effect likened to drunkenness, brought about by the depth and the nitrogen he was breathing. It had been creeping up on him for several minutes, but he had shrugged off the danger signals.

Now it was too late. His numbed brain saw what was happening and signaled his limbs, but they refused to respond. He was frozen on the spot.

Adams raised the knife to his airline and sliced through it neatly. The water rushed into Adams' helmet, distorting his face. He formed a circle with his thumb and first finger and signaled to Darrow that all was O.K.

When Darrow reached him, it was too late. Not that he could have helped anyway. When Adams cut the airline, there was no power on earth that could have saved him.

CHAPTER TWENTY-FIVE

Adams had crumpled slowly to the deck of the *Mary Owen* and now Darrow took the silent body in his arms. He wished he could have said something, anything. Adams had sacrificed his own life so that the others might live and Darrow hadn't even been able to let the man know how he felt.

Anger boiled up within him. Anger at Hayama, anger at himself, anger at the world and all the greed that lurked within the hearts of those that lived on its surface. He wanted to scream, to cry, but he could do neither.

Ten seconds ago the best friend he had in the world had breathed his last. The only thing left now was revenge. Sooner or later it would be his and it would be sweet. Oh God, it would be sweet. So sweet.

An explosion shook the water, pounding at his

eardrums and intestines. His nose started to bleed and the face mask began to fill with the thick redness. He looked up toward the surface and the hull of the *Malacca Maid* seemed to disintegrate before his eyes. Hayama must have hit the fuel tank with his machine gun.

Bits of rubble began to fall into the water with a silent ripple and the Darrow watched helplessly as the *Maid* began to settle toward him.

He sat frozen, unable to move as the ship sank slowly past him and disappeared from view into the never-ending depths of the crevasse. With luck someone might have survived. If they had, they would need his help.

He released Adams and the First Mate settled gently on to the wreck. Darrow looked at him for one last time and started for the surface.

"Here lies old Bart Adams," he thought. "A friend of all whores and madams."

He surfaced quickly, disregarding the decompression stops. With any luck, he would have three to six hours before he was forced to resubmerge and take time out for decompression. He broke water in the center of a large circle of floating debris and oil. Pushing the face mask high on his forehead, he looked around quickly.

One of the life boats from the *Malacca Maid* floated upside down a few yards away. In the near area, he could see the mast, a few life jackets and shattered bits of the hull bobbing atop the water.

He felt the searing pain in his left shoulder before he heard the shot. He spun around in the water just in time to see the black hull of Hayama's junk bearing down on him. Someone was standing on the bow triggering a Thompson.

He tried frantically to dive, but it was too late. The side of the junk hit him with a bone jarring force and he was knocked away and then sucked under and dragged along the hull. The pounding of the propeller grated in his ears.

He jackknifed in the water, his feet seeking the bow of the junk. He found it and kicked it with all his strength, shooting his body away from the junk. Then he was sucked back in and the propellers clanged loudly against the SCUBA tanks on his back.

The junk was completely by and he was being tossed about like a cork in its boiling wake. He was conscious, but that was about all.

He knew they would be back for another run at him and his mind groped frantically for a lifesaving solution.

He was five or six feet below the surface and he stayed there, too weak to dive any deeper. Another pass with the junk and he would be dead. His searching eyes found and locked on the half-submerged lifeboat a few feet away. He swam to it weakly and surfaced beneath it just as the junk sped by a second time. He grabbed a seat and hung on as the lifeboat tossed in the wake.

Suddenly he was aware that he wasn't alone and he turned slowly, half dazed. There was just enough light under the boat so that he could make out the features of O'Mally. The man moaned and Darrow thanked God that he was still alive. He spoke softly in an attempt to encourage the other man, not knowing if he was being heard. Then he touched O'Mally and was immediately sorry for it.

The man screamed in agony and Darrow's heart sank as he wondered if the scream had been heard aboard the junk. If it had, the end was pretty damn close.

The junk roared by again in its search for Darrow and the lifeboat bobbed in the water, allowing just a bit of light to seep under the boat. It was then that Darrow saw why O'Mally had screamed so horribly.

His face was a blackened, swollen mass of burned flesh. The skin had broken open in great, wide cracks baring the raw flesh a quarter of an inch deep.

Darrow felt for his face mask and breathed a sigh of relief when he found it to be still there. He pulled it down and dropped a foot or two beneath the surface.

When he came back up, he was sick. O'Mally's whole body was in the same condition as his face. Darrow marveled at the fact that he was still alive. In this condition, death would be merciful. The sooner it came, the better. By the time the junk had made a few more passes over the area and roared away in the direction of the atoll, it was all over for O'Mally.

Darrow had partly recovered from his brush with the junk by this time and he ducked out from under the lifeboat. This time he searched the sea in all directions before he relaxed. It had been too close for comfort before.

He cut the wet suit away from his injured shoulder and examined the wound. Fortunately it wasn't bad. A shallow gash in the fleshy part of his upper arm. The salt water had stopped the bleeding and he felt that it would give him no trouble.

It was then that he first noticed the pains in his shoulder and knee joints. The bends had come on faster than he anticipated. There was no getting around it. He was going to have to dive.

He looked at the junk and saw it was slowly disappearing around the atoll. He hoped Vargas and Elizabeth would give up without a fight. They would be no match for Hayama and if they could stay alive for a while, Darrow might be able to help them. Even as he thought this, he heard the shots. He cursed himself for having left a forty-five at the camp. He should have known better.

Checking the pressure gauge, Darrow found he had air left for about two hours. It wasn't near as much time as he would have liked to have, but it would have to do. He dropped down to thirty feet and prepared to sit it out. It was destined to be the longest two hours in his life.

While he waited, he thought of Elizabeth and vowed to kill any man that laid a hand on her. He knew now that he loved her and only wished that he had been able to tell her before he left that morning. If he had to die, that would somehow make it easier.

Thinking now of his crew, he felt he should say a few words over their watery grave, but knew of nothing to say. He cursed himself as a poor Skipper that had sacrificed his crew for greed. True, each man had volunteered, but he had led them. Their deaths would have to be placed on his shoulders. The ironic fact remained that all but the first two gold bars had been carried to the bottom of the crevasse. There was no hope at all for recovery.

The gold that they had raised the day before, had been left on the atoll and by this time, Darrow figured Hayama would be drooling over it greedily. If Darrow had his way, he wouldn't drool long. Maybe he would die happy, though.

He checked his watch again and swore when he found he had only been down fifteen minutes. It had felt like a dozen life times.

The pain in his joints had subsided somewhat and he pondered with the idea of saying the hell with decompression and surfacing. He decided against it almost immediately. He would be no good to Elizabeth dead, but he hated to think of all that could happen to her in the hour and forty-five minutes he had left. Knowing Hayama like he did, he felt he could expect the worst.

As he waited, he began to swim slowly toward the atoll. He would have to cover the distance sooner or later anyway and it would save time to do it while waiting out the decompression period.

In thirty minutes, he was sitting on the bottom in about thirty-five feet of water. The atoll rose above the surface less than a hundred feet away and Darrow had to fight down the impulse to surface for a quick look.

It would do him no harm physically, but if they saw him, he would have lost a valuable advantage. As it was, Hayama undoubtedly believed him dead.

He rested a few minutes and then began to circle the atoll. Looking up at the surface, he saw the sky was a bright blue. He would have liked to try and work his way into the center of the atoll and sit under the junk in case Hayama decided to pull out. He discarded the idea as being too risky. The water was clear as a bell in there and with the sky this blue, he was sure to be spotted.

As it was, he stopped just off the channel and allowed himself to sink to the bottom. A whole hour to go yet. God! He wished he could do something! A few minutes short of an hour later, his air supply ran out and he was forced to surface. The decompression time was less than half of that recommended, but he could only hope it was time enough.

He crawled ashore by the high rock at the tip of the atoll and squirmed forward on his stomach until he was well into the Masabate grass. He climbed quietly out of the SCUBA tanks and wet suit and lay back on the grass to relax for the first time in several hours. In looking around, he saw that it was the same place he and Elizabeth had come the other night.

He closed his eyes and thought longingly of the events that night. If he only could have known then what was about to take place. If only he had it to do over again. He didn't, however, and there was no sense crying over spilled milk.

His outstretched hand brushed something and he opened his eyes to find a crumpled, half empty pack of cigarettes. He must have dropped them the other night. "Maybe my luck is turning," he thought. They were just what the doctor had ordered. He could have used a good stiff shot to better advantage, but he took what was available and was happy with it.

They had been wet from the last night's rain and

the paper was yellow and close to falling apart. He picked out a good one and stuck it shakily in his mouth, fumbling for matches with his free hand. Of course, he didn't have any. To a heavy smoker, there is but one thing worse than being out of cigarettes and that is to have them and be out of matches.

He swore, half aloud, and searched his brain for a solution. He thought of chewing the damn things but decided against it. Then he saw the lantern. His underwater lantern was still hooked to the bottom of the SCUBA lung and he reached for it hurriedly, an idea forming in his mind.

With shaking hands, he unscrewed the front rim and the lens dropped out. He rolled to his belly and jutted his chin out so that the sun would hit the cigarette. Then he placed the lens between it and the sun, the center part concentrating right on the tip. It began to smoke in a few seconds and he puffed on it hungrily, sucking the pleasure filled smoke deep into his lungs. Satisfied, be rolled to his back and cushioning his head with one arm, stared thoughtfully at the solid blue of the skies. He had a hell of a job ahead of him and didn't have the faintest idea where to start.

He had no idea how many men Hayama had after the battle in which the *Malacca Maid* was sunk. As near as he could estimate, Hayama had lost four men in their gun battle of several days ago. He most likely had started with a crew of fifteen. Nothing definite to the contrary, Darrow would still have to figure there were eleven left. He had seen better odds. A hell of a lot better odds.

As he lay there a plan began to formulate slowly. He was banking desperately on Hayama spending at least one night on the atoll. To carry out his plan, it was imperative that he have the cover of darkness. Darkness and one hell of a lot of luck. He snubbed out the cigarette and, moving slowly on his stomach, made his way to the edge of the Masabate grass where he could overlook the camp.

The junk was rocking gently at anchor within the protective circle of the atoll. A few yards away, Darrow's old camp, now partly torn down, was the center of activity. Darrow searched the area anxiously for Elizabeth and finally spotted her at the base of one of the larger trees on the far side of camp. Her clothing was torn, revealing completely one white breast. Her hair was in disarray and her face was smudged with dirt. Darrow clenched his fists tightly and muffled a curse. Someone would pay for this.

Beside Elizabeth, Peter Vargas sat with his hands bound behind his back. From all outward appearance, he had been roughed up also.

Hayama was nowhere in sight, but Darrow counted seven of his henchmen including his captain, Pedro Sanches. Once again the anger boiled up within him and he fought to hold it down.

Quietly, he began to inch his way back into the Masabate, still on his stomach and moving backward a fraction of an inch at a time so as not to rustle the grass.

He was almost all of the way back in when someone grabbed his hair, yanking his head back hard. A long-bladed knife flashed before his eyes and he winced as the cold steel was pressed hard against his throat. Cold beads of sweat broke out on his forehead and for a second, he was frozen with fear. Even his instinctive will to fight had failed him this time.

A voice mumbled cruelly in Chinese and warned him that the slightest move would send the steel plunging into his throat. From the tone of the voice, Darrow felt the man would like nothing better. He didn't move a muscle.

A knee dug hard into the center of his back and the pressure on his hair increased, forcing his head back roughly. The knife pressed harder against his throat and he felt a thin trickle of blood running down onto his chest. Whoever this joker was, he meant business.

A second man moved around to the front of him and Darrow looked angrily at a pair of sinewy bare legs. Then, one of the legs lashed out quickly and the wooden sandal caught him squarely between the eyes. He barely saw it as it lashed out at him the second and third times and after that, he saw or felt nothing, although the action was repeated several times.

CHAPTER TWENTY-SIX

The first thing he saw when he opened his eyes was her face. It was Elizabeth and she bent close to him, half whispering, half sobbing in his ear.

"John! Oh, John, please! Say something. Say something!"

"I love you, Elizabeth. I love you. I wanted so badly to tell you. I was afraid for a while that I wasn't going to get the chance. Now that I have, now that you know, nothing matters."

"Oh, John, I'm so glad to hear you say that, but you're wrong. You're so wrong. Everything matters now." She lifted his head in her arms and cuddled his face against her bare breast. "A few minutes ago I didn't care what they did to me. I thought you were dead. I had nothing to live for. Now I have everything. We'll let them have the gold and we'll go somewhere, anywhere. Now that we have each other, we don't need gold. Our wealth is in each other."

Darrow was still dazed and he struggled to thrash away the fog that cloaked his brain. She was right. He had to live now. He had to live to keep her alive.

She tore away a portion of her blouse and rushed to the beach, dipping it in the surf. Returning, she took his head in her arms again and began to frantically wipe at the blood and dirt that covered his face. She paled, but said nothing when the wounds were exposed. The cold cloth felt wonderfully refreshing for a second and then the salt in the water began to eat at the raw flesh and Darrow muffled a groan, clenching his lips between his teeth.

When she had finished, she helped him to a sitting position and Darrow shook his head in an attempt to clear the cobwebs that still lingered there. In an effort to move his arms, he discovered that he, like Vargas, was bound hand and foot.

Suto Hayama stood talking quietly to Pedro Sanches only a few yards away and when he saw that Darrow was conscious, he strutted over cockily.

Watching Darrow's face closely, he smiled crookedly

and lighted a long, black cheroot. The jagged scar on his face twisted his mouth into a distorted sneer as he sucked deep on the smoke and blew it in Darrow's direction. "You're a very clever man, Captain Darrow, but as you can see, I am the more clever of the two. If you are as wise as I believe you to be, you will realize immediately that it will be best if you tell us everything we want to know."

Darrow snarled and spit into the dust at Hayama's feet. "Like what?"

"I think you know very well, Captain. So far we have found but two bars of the gold. A goodly amount to be sure and more than enough to satisfy me, but I think you'll agree when I tell you I have a rather greedy crew. If you tell us where you have hidden the rest of it, I will see that you and the young lady are deposited safely in the Philippines."

Pedro Sanches stood at his side and laughed harshly. Darrow noticed with pleasure that his face and bare chest was covered with scar tissue from the burns he suffered when Darrow blew up the two junks.

"Those two bars are the only ones left," Darrow said. "You sent almost twelve million dollars to the bottom when you sank the *Malacca Maid*. There isn't anybody on earth that can get at it now."

Hayama swore and threw the cheroot to the ground, grinding it into the dirt with an angry twist of his sandaled foot. "You're not dealing with fools, Captain." He hesitated a moment, lowering his head and staring thoughtfully at the ground. "If I were the type to be philosophical, I would tell you that it is better to live in poverty than to die in wealth."

Darrow shrugged his shoulders and stared directly at Hayama. Then an idea struck him. He was quiet for a while, mulling it over in his mind. The more he thought about it, the better it seemed. It wasn't a sure-fire solution, but it was worth a try. "All right, Hayama, I'll make you a deal. Put Vargas and Miss McClain ashore in the Philippines and bring back proof to me that you have done so. When I have that proof, I'll show you where we buried the rest of the gold. I'll make no other deals."

Elizabeth cast a startled look at Darrow and got hurriedly to her feet. "Don't believe him. Can you understand, there is no more gold. He was telling the truth."

Hayama looked at Darrow, waiting for his reply to Elizabeth's statement.

"It's no good, Elizabeth," Darrow said. "Hayama is right. A hell of a lot of good the gold will do us if we're buried alongside of it." Darrow was lying, stalling for time. If he could only get Hayama to free Elizabeth, he would worry about himself when the time came.

Hayama stared at Darrow and fingered the scar on the side of his face. "You must think me to be a fool, Captain. Once I freed Miss McClain, she would have the authorities down here to rescue you before I could get halfway back. Now that you have confirmed my thoughts about more gold being on the atoll, I'm sure we have ways of making you tell where it is."

Darrow winced and his heart fell. Hayama knew what he was talking about. His men could get blood out of a turnip and have fun doing it.

Sanches pulled a knife from his belt and ran his

fingers lightly over the cutting edge. He looked at Elizabeth and Darrow could guess what he had on his mind.

"Not her," Hayama said. "We'll start with Mr. Vargas."

To this point, Vargas had been staring despondently at the ground, listening to the talk, but saying nothing. Now his head jerked up and his eyes were wild with fear. "Not me, Suto. For God's sake, not me. I'm your friend. I put you on to this gold in the first place. You can have my share. Do what you want with them, but for God's sake, let me go. I'm in this as deep as you are," he sobbed. "You know I can't go to the police."

Darrow looked at Elizabeth's uncle sharply. So he had been the one. The pieces were beginning to fall into place. Vargas must have discovered his brother-in-law's secret some time ago. He had tried to lay his hands on the log page back in San Francisco when Elizabeth's home was searched and then again on the ship when the steward was murdered. Failing both times, he had enlisted the aid of Hayama to take the page by force that night in Macao. When that failed, he had struck out on his own, but Hayama, too, was determined to get at the gold. It had been a kind of double double-cross.

Elizabeth gasped and looked at her uncle in amazement. "Uncle Peter," she cried. "You, you, how could you? If you needed money, you would have only had to ask."

Vargas didn't even hear her. His terror-stricken eyes never left the knife in Sanches' hand.

"Part of it wasn't enough," Darrow said. "He wanted it all. All or nothing. When he joined hands with Suto

Hayama, he signed his own death warrant. They're two of a kind."

Elizabeth buried her face in her hands and began to cry softly, her body shaking with each sob.

Hayama spit disgustedly at Vargas and motioned to Sanches.

Sanches called in Chinese to two of his men and they lifted the struggling Vargas to his feet. Once there, they slashed the ropes that bound his hands and, stretching his arms high overhead, tied them to one of the palm trees. His flailing legs were caught and yanked down, then tied at the base of the tree. His body was stretched painfully along the trunk. A second later the clothes were slashed from him.

Darrow knew what was coming and he felt that even Vargas didn't deserve it, but he was powerless to stop it. Vargas was going to be a pawn in the game of death.

There was a piercing, chilling scream from Vargas' trembling lips and Darrow looked away. In a second, it was all over and he looked back.

Vargas was still alive, but it would have been better for him had he not been. A quick, thin slash had been made from side to side across his stomach with the razor-sharp knife and his intestines had tumbled out, spilling down the front of his legs and hanging almost to the ground. His body trembled convulsively and he screamed again.

It was amazing what punishment the human body could stand.

Elizabeth screamed and collapsed limply to the ground.

Hayama's men stopped whatever they had been doing and gathered around in a half circle to watch the proceedings. Now and then they would laugh and point out something that amused them.

The smile never left Sanches' face as he calmly wiped the thin trace of blood from his knife and replaced it in his belt.

Hayama looked on with satisfaction and said to Sanches, "Let him alone for the time being. We have plenty of time. Let them spend the night like this and listen to his cries and then let them listen to his final death throes. In the morning, they will be quite happy to tell us where the gold is buried."

CHAPTER TWENTY-SEVEN

Darrow looked at the ground and fought to keep from throwing up. Unless they did something, they would never leave the atoll. Now they had been given one break, however. They would be left alone throughout the night. If they were still prisoners in the morning, they would meet the same fate that Vargas had. He leaned back against the tree and half closed his eyes, watching them through the thin slits. In a few minutes, they lost interest in Vargas and went back to whatever they had been doing.

Every few seconds Vargas would shudder convulsively and scream. Darrow tried not to listen.

The time until dark passed slowly. Elizabeth stayed where she had fallen, moving slightly from time to time and now and then a faint, "No! No!" would escape from her lips. Her fainting spell had fallen off into a troubled, half sleep. It would be better if she remained that way until Vargas died.

The ropes that bound Darrow's hands behind him were tight, numbing his arms and cutting into his wrists whenever he attempted to move. When the pirates began preparing their evening meal, the aroma of steaming rice drifted past his nostrils and set his stomach into angry motion. He had had nothing to eat or drink since early that morning and his lips, too, were dry and parched, his tongue beginning to swell slightly in his mouth.

Not fearing Elizabeth, Hayama had not bound her during the day and Darrow was hopeful that they would leave her that way throughout the night. Immediately after dinner, however, she too was trussed up and thrown against the tree beside him. Then the saki was brought out and the crew of the junk began to gulp it down thirstily, certain they were rich men and talking wildly about their plans for their shares of the gold.

This was what Darrow had hoped for. They had rechecked his bonds and finding them secure, had begun to relax. It would make it easier later on when Darrow made his play.

Elizabeth came to at about ten o'clock and began to sob convulsively again. Darrow nudged her and whispered she should be quiet. It was a touchy situation and Darrow wanted to attract as little attention as possible.

The men were good and drunk by this time and with luck, they would completely forget Darrow and

Elizabeth. If for some reason or other they were reminded, however, there was no telling what games they might devise with their captives. Elizabeth understood and the sobbing stopped. He marveled at how well she was able to pull herself together. If she had snapped, it would have made escape almost impossible.

Darrow began working feverishly at his bonds. After an hour, they were no looser than they had been before. He doubled his legs under him and edged his way closer to Elizabeth. She dropped to her side and began pulling at the knots with her teeth, but they were pulled too tight. They would have to find another way.

He helped her back to a sitting position and tried pulling at them until the sweat ran down his brow and the blood began to trickle from the wounds that the ropes had rubbed raw. He was ready to give up when he saw something at the end of his outstretched legs. It was Vargas' belt buckle. When they had stripped him, it had been torn free and now it could be the instrument that would save them.

He stretched his legs until he touched it with the ends of his bare feet. Then he began to pull it in slowly. In five minutes, he had it clenched tightly in his hands. His fingers were numb and stiff and it was not easy to tell if he was making any headway, but he kept at it. Presently, he felt some loosening and when he tugged sharply, they came free.

He looked at his watch and found it to be almost one o'clock in the morning. He tugged hastily at the ropes that held his feet and, in a few minutes, they too were free. Next he freed Elizabeth, cautioning her to leave her hands behind her back. Now they would only have to wait for the right moment!

Most of the men had passed out by this time. They lay sprawled here and there about the camp. Only Sanches and two others were yet awake.

Hayama had taken the two bars of gold aboard the junk earlier in the evening and had not returned. Chances were he was in the middle of a good drunk himself.

Vargas hadn't moved or made a sound for some time, but now he came to life in a sudden and final convulsion. A harsh rattle rose from his throat and then died off in a choking sound. His head dropped loosely to his chest and Darrow knew he would suffer no more.

The sound of Vargas' death alerted Sanches and he left the other two men and staggered over. He looked at the body and chuckled, then broke into a throaty laugh. Finally, into a drunken roar that shook his body.

The other two men looked up briefly, smiled at each other and went back to their drinking.

Sanches turned to walk away, then stopped and started back. His eyes fell on Elizabeth and it didn't take much of a prophet to tell what he was thinking.

He bent and cupped one of her exposed breasts in a grimy hand and made a soft, cooing sound with his mouth. He dropped to one knee and that's when Darrow hit him. He brought his left hand around from behind his back and caught Sanches on the side of the neck with a judo chop. Sanches tumbled to the dirt, but the blow had missed its mark and he bounded back quickly to his feet, his hand fumbling for the knife at his belt.

Darrow was on him before he could draw it clear and the two men fell back to the ground. They rolled back into the trees and as yet, Sanches had not made a sound. Darrow found his throat with one hand and with the other hand, searched for the knife. His fingers closed on it and he pulled it from Sanches' belt, then drove it with all his strength into the man's chest.

Sanches screamed and then went limp, but it was like dropping a bomb on the silent camp. Men were up all over the place, staggering dazedly in all directions.

Elizabeth was on her feet now and Darrow pushed her behind him. He pulled the knife from Sanches' body and waited. He didn't have long to wait.

Someone rushed blindly at him in the darkness of the trees and Darrow drove the knife to the hilt in the man's belly. He ran his hands quickly over the body and found what he was looking for. A German Luger tucked into the waist band. Probably a wartime relic.

He took Elizabeth's hand and crouching down, broke into the open at a dead run.

Someone loomed up before him and he fired once with the Luger, spinning the man around and dropping him in his tracks. They skirted his body and continued on toward the inner circle of the atoll, still running hard.

Behind them, someone yelled and a shot rang out, then another. Darrow pulled Elizabeth to the ground just as someone cut loose with a sub-machine gun.

He hit the ground flat on his belly and twisted around, keeping his body between Elizabeth and the camp. Someone was silhouetted against the light of the fire and Darrow took quick aim and fired. The man threw his arms into the air and pitched backward into the burning logs.

Darrow fired twice more, counting his shots, and then started once more for the beach. He bad four rounds left. He would have to make every one count.

Elizabeth hit the water first with Darrow hard on her heels. He held the Luger over his head and struck out for the junk with his free arm. Behind them, there was more shooting and waterspouts began to form around them as the slugs plowed into the lagoon.

They skirted the junk and came up on the side opposite the camp. "I'll go up first," he whispered. "Hayama is on board and maybe someone else. When I clear them out, I'll toss you a rope. Are you all right so far?"

"I'm fine. Just be careful. We're too close now to let anything happen."

Ashore, someone fired again with a sub-machine gun and Darrow heard Hayama yelling excitedly from the deck above them. He would have to work fast before they realized what was happening. He found the anchor chain and started up hand over hand, the Luger clenched in his teeth. He reached the rail and dropped over silently, then moved to the shadows of the cabin. Someone popped out of a door almost on top of him and Darrow struck out with the barrel of the automatic. He connected solidly and the figure dropped like a sack of wheat.

Darrow ran his hands over the person in search of another weapon, recoiled when he touched bare skin, then swore when his fumbling hands discovered it was a woman. He might have known that the bastard would have a woman with him, but this was the first time he was aware of it. That would explain Hayama's reason for staying on the junk instead of getting drunk ashore. The woman was stark naked and Darrow might have let his hands linger longer than was necessary.

In a moment, he stood up again and continued along the side of the cabin. He came to the end of it and turned the corner to find Hayama facing away from him, yelling orders to the shore. "Stop right there, Suto. Make one move and you're a dead man," he said.

Hayama spun around and dropped to one knee. A pistol blazed in his hand and splinters flew from the cabin beside Darrow's head. He fired twice in return, but missed both times, then he edged back around the side of the cabin. He would have to make the next two shots count.

Hayama yelled to the men ashore that Darrow was aboard the junk and they splashed drunkenly into the water. Darrow would have to pull Elizabeth aboard in one hell of a hurry.

He dived forward, landing on his belly and then rolling quickly to one side. He came to rest belly down and steadied the Luger with both hands. Hayama stood with his back to the rail and fired again, but missed.

Darrow took his time and then triggered the automatic twice, both slugs ripping into Hayama's mid-section. The man collapsed and rolled under the rail into the water.

Bounding to his feet, Darrow darted to the rail where Elizabeth was waiting. He tossed a line into the water and yelled for her to grab hold. A few seconds later, she was on deck beside him. "Get into the cabin and stay there," he said. "I'm going to start the engines. With any luck, we'll be out of this damned mess in about two minutes!"

She did as he directed and Darrow dashed to the helm. He groped for the automatic starter, found it, and pressed with a trembling finger. His lips formed a silent prayer for the first time in as long as he could remember.

The engines groaned, turned over twice, sputtered and died. He swore and pressed the starter again. This time they roared to life. Quickly, he engaged the clutch and the junk lurched forward. It was too sudden though, and the engines died again.

Still swearing, he restarted them and revved to full power before letting them die off. Then, he engaged the clutch once more and they were under way.

There was more firing from shore and Darrow could hear the deadly whistle as the angry slugs passed overhead. He heard the slap as some of them dug into the cabin and hull of the junk.

He turned the bow in what he hoped was the direction of the channel and crossed his fingers. Half way through the coral scraped hard against the port side and for a second, he thought they were aground. Then she broke loose and they pushed into the open sea.

Darrow relaxed and leaned weakly against the wheel. His body was covered with a clammy sweat and his knees were shaking to the point where he wondered about their ability to hold him up. He still couldn't believe they had made it.

He turned the bow into the southeast and let her nose head on into the rising swells. Looking at the sky, he saw that a storm was brewing. "Let her blow," he thought. "Let her blow her guts out."

It was just before noon when the junk nosed into a small harbor on the southern tip of Zamboanga. The man and woman at the helm stood quietly side by side until her port side rubbed against the pier.

The dock attendant snubbed the bowline to a piling and then stared in amused wonderment as the two figures locked themselves in each other's arms.

"You would think they'd wait until they got to the hotel," he said to a man at his side.

THE END

Conrad William (Bill)
Dawn was born on
December 9, 1933 in San
Francisco. His family then
moved to Los Angeles and
Portland. He joined the
Marines in the Signal Corp
in 1951 and was wounded in
action in Korea in 1953.

Dawn traveled around the world and was at various
times a sailor, a fighter and a newspaper man. He
wrote six men's adventure novels, all for Novel
Books in the early 1960s. He was married three
times, eventually settling in Phoenix, Arizona. Dawn
died there in Ajo, Arizona, on November 12, 2002.